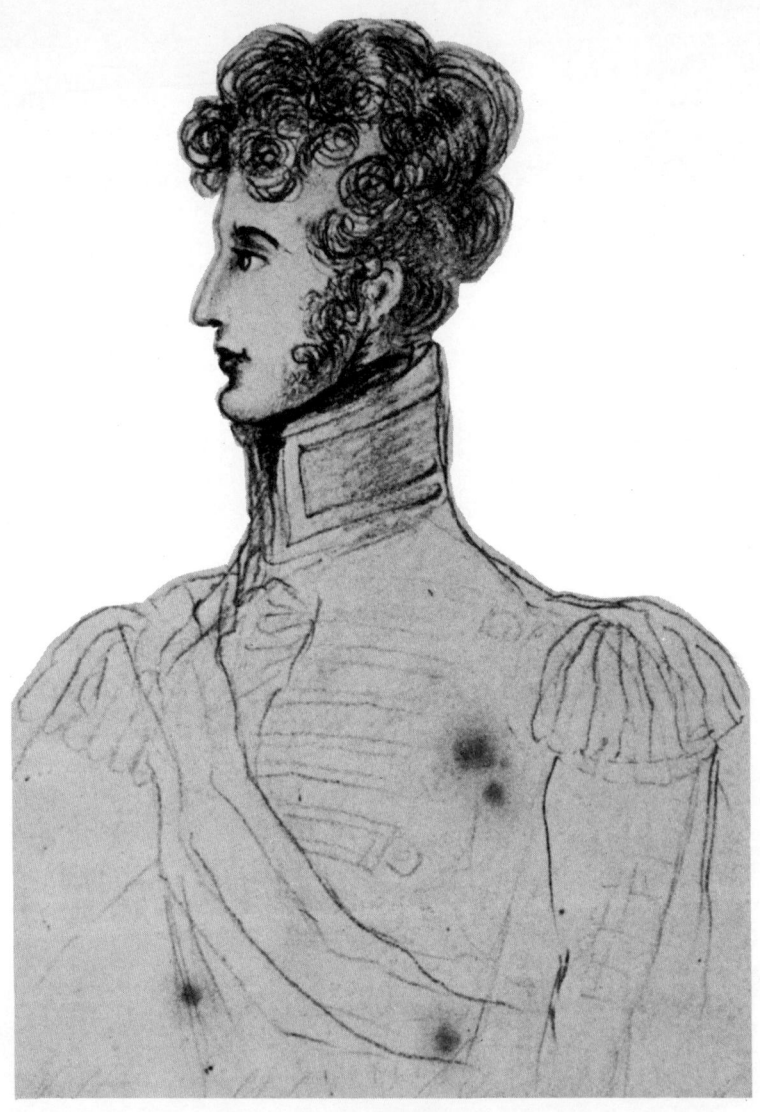

Arthur Wellesley

Marquis of Douro and Duke of Zamorna.
Pencil drawing by Charlotte Brontë.

Something about Arthur

by

CHARLOTTE BRONTË

Transcribed from the Original Manuscript
and Edited by
CHRISTINE ALEXANDER

Humanities Research Center

THE UNIVERSITY OF TEXAS AT AUSTIN

Copyright © 1981 by the Humanities Research Center
The University of Texas at Austin
ISBN 0-87959-095-5

Frontispiece: Head of Arthur, Marquis of Douro. This drawing and the watercolor of Mina Laury on pg. 8 are reproduced by courtesy of the Brontë Society.

TO MY PARENTS
BRUCE AND JUNE BAIRD

CONTENTS

Introduction	9
The Text: "Something about Arthur"	31
Explanatory Notes	60
Deletions and Corrections in the Manuscript	63
Alterations of Punctuation	71
Location of Manuscripts by Charlotte and Patrick Branwell Brontë Referred to in the Introduction and Notes	74

Mina Laury

A watercolor by Charlotte Brontë
after W. Finden's engraving of
"The Maid of Saragoza."

INTRODUCTION

"I have now written a great many books—" Charlotte Brontë noted in 1839, "& for a long time I have dwelt on the same characters & scenes & subjects— I have shewn my landscapes in every variety of shade & light— which morning, noon & evening — the rising — the meridian & the setting sun can bestow upon them."[1] One of these books was "Something about Arthur," a thirteen-page romance written when she was seventeen. The work provided Charlotte Brontë with a context in which to develop her characters, scenes, and subjects, as well as her style. It is an important document of her literary apprenticeship.

The provenance of "Something about Arthur" is fairly well established. It was probably part of a "curious packet . . . containing an immense amount of manuscript, in an inconceivably small space; tales, dramas, poems, romances, written principally by Charlotte, in a hand which it is almost impossible to decipher without the aid of a magnifying glass."[2] This packet of manuscripts first left Haworth in 1856 in the care of Mrs. Elizabeth Gaskell, who was writing a biography of Charlotte Brontë, dead the previous year.

Obtaining material for this biography was difficult. The Reverend Patrick Brontë, Charlotte's father, although helpful was intimidating. Furthermore, Charlotte's husband, the Reverend Arthur Bell Nicholls, had inherited most of the needed manuscripts. Still mourning Charlotte's death, he was reluctant to have his brief married life exposed to the world. Had it not been for Sir James Kay-Shuttleworth, the philanthropist and would-be friend of Charlotte, "Something about Arthur" and other manuscripts of Brontë juvenilia might never have been brought to early public

---

[1] From the Brontë Parsonage Museum manuscript: B125(1); see also Thomas James Wise and John Alexander Symington, eds., *The Miscellaneous and Unpublished Writings of Charlotte and Patrick Branwell Brontë* [The Shakespeare Head Brontë], vol. 2 (Oxford: Basil Blackwell, 1938), p. 403.

[2] Mrs. Gaskell, *The Life of Charlotte Brontë*, 3rd ed., rev. (London: Smith, Elder, 1857), vol. 1 pp. 88–9.

attention through Mrs. Gaskell's biography. Sir James unexpectedly accompanied Mrs. Gaskell on her visit to the Haworth parsonage and, according to her, "coolly took actual possession of many things while Mr. Nicholls was saying he could not possibly part with them." Mrs. Gaskell, somewhat embarrassed, "came away with the 'Professor' the beginning of her new tale 'Emma'—about 10 pages written in the finest pencil writing, —& by far the most extraordinary of all, a packet about the size of a lady's travelling writing case, full of paper books of different sizes . . . all in this indescribably fine writing."[3]

Mrs. Gaskell was not able to read all the manuscripts and so was unaware of their interconnection and larger significance in relation to Charlotte's later novels. She was, however, the first person to recognize Charlotte's juvenilia as her literary apprenticeship. Furthermore, she published a facsimile page of an early manuscript and transcribed several other manuscripts "as a curious proof how early the rage for literary composition had seized upon" Charlotte Brontë.[4]

This "quantity of fragments" was returned to Mr. Nicholls after Mrs. Gaskell had rewritten about forty pages of the biography. Following Mr. Brontë's death, Mr. Nicholls took the parcel of manuscripts with him to his own home in Banagher, Ireland. For nearly thirty years, "Something about Arthur" and the rest of the manuscripts in the parcel lay "in the bottom of a cupboard tied up in a newspaper."[5]

On 31 March 1895 Thomas James Wise, through the agency of Clement Shorter, purchased this parcel along with many other Brontë manuscripts. Wise brought many of the manuscripts to public attention through references in *A Bibliography of the Writings in Prose and Verse of Members of the Brontë Family* (London, 1917). He regrouped the manuscripts and had many of them handsomely bound in red, green, and brown morocco. After retaining some for his own library, he dispersed the rest in private sales amongst collectors and friends. Pages of stories were detached and lost. Many of the manuscripts were published privately —heavily abridged and inaccurately transcribed—in expensive limited editions. Some were taken abroad, including "Something about Arthur,"

---

[3] Mrs. Gaskell to George Smith, 25 July 1856; J.A.V. Chapple and Arthur Pollard, eds., *The Letters of Mrs. Gaskell* (Manchester: Manchester University Press, 1966), p. 398.

[4] *The Life of Charlotte Brontë*, vol. 1, p. 89.

[5] Clement Shorter, *Charlotte Brontë and Her Circle* (London: Hodder and Stoughton, 1896), p. 25.

which was offered for sale in 1952 by James F. Drake, a New York antiquarian bookseller. The manuscript was bought that December by H. J. Lutcher Stark, at the suggestion of Fannie E. Ratchford, Librarian of the Rare Books Collection of the University of Texas at Austin. In January 1977, "Something about Arthur" was donated to the Humanities Research Center by the Nelda C. and H.J. Lutcher Stark Foundation.

THE EARLY BRONTË JUVENILIA

Although "Something about Arthur" was written in 1833 after Charlotte Brontë had returned home from her studies at Roe Head school, the characters, settings, and subjects had been developing as early as 1826 through the imaginary dramas which she and her brother and sisters created and acted out. Characters in the "Plays," as the Brontë children called them, came from fairy stories, local legends, reports in newspapers, and overheard conversations; the plays were continually elaborated on as they were acted out. Three years later Charlotte began to chronicle the events and characters of these plays on tiny scraps of paper. She was then thirteen years old. These early manuscripts as well as Branwell's detailed corroborative accounts document the development of the Brontës's imaginative childhood world.

In "The History of the Year," written on 12 March 1829, Charlotte described the three main plays: the "Young Men's Play," "Our Fellows," and "The Islanders." The "Young Men's Play" began when Mr. Brontë, returning home on 5 June 1826 from a clerical conference in Leeds, brought Branwell a set of twelve wooden toy soldiers. Immediately the children each chose a favorite soldier, endowed it with an imaginary life, and began to weave around it a fairy-tale world. Charlotte named her soldier the Duke of Wellington, after her father's hero; Branwell called his Bonaparte, although he later changed the name to Sneaky. By comparison, Emily's "Gravey" and Anne's "Waiting Boy" seemed unheroic. Their feeble names were soon changed to Parry and Ross, two famous explorers who made more suitable companions for Wellington and Bonaparte.

In all Charlotte's and Branwell's stories, however, Parry and Ross were given a secondary role. It is not surprising that in 1831 the two younger sisters broke away to form their own imaginary world of Gondal. They took no further part in Charlotte's and Branwell's plays, and, from this time on, the early literary partnerships in the Brontë family were clearly defined. Emily's diary paper of 26 June 1837[6] shows that the children were aware of each other's writing, but Emily's Gondal story, despite some resemblance to the early plays, bore no obvious relationship to Charlotte's and Branwell's later literary creations of Glass Town and Angria.

"A Romantic Tale," Charlotte's first story about the twelve Young Men, is dated 15 April 1829 and describes the Young Men's voyage from England to the east coast of Africa, their struggles with the Ashantee natives, and their settlement and building of Glass Town. Reminiscent of the *Arabian Nights*, this African kingdom was ruled by four Chief Genii, played by the Brontë children themselves, the latter directing the course of events as well as the movements of their particular characters.

The children became both creators of the play and creators within the play. Their characters based on real people developed a reality of their own; literature was produced by and about these make-believe characters, while more literature was produced about the whole play. Levels of reality became blurred and make-believe characters even questioned the reality of their make-believe world. One of Charlotte's characters, for example, was astonished to find that he was merely a figment of his creator's imagination: "It seemed as if I was a non-existent shadow—that I neither spoke, eat [sic], imagined, or lived of myself, but I was the mere idea of some other creature's brain. The Glass Town seemed so likewise."[7]

From its earliest stages the children's imaginary land had a geography which was carefully and thoroughly documented, lending verisimilitude to the Glass Town stories. Branwell's detailed folding map in "The History of the Young Men" illustrates the kingdoms founded by the children's four chief characters. The Great Glass Town, situated on the Great Bay where the River Guadima (or "Guadiana" as it is called in "Something about Arthur") meets the River Niger, is the center of this federation of states. As the stories progress the name of the federal capital becomes more sophisticated: it changes first to Verreopolis, which "means the Glass Town being compounded of a Greek & French word to that effect,"[8] and is then corrupted to Verdopolis. Descriptions of the various

---

[6] *Brontë Society Transactions*, vol. 12, part 61 (1951): 15.
[7] *Miscellaneous and Unpublished Writings*, vol. 1 (1936), p. 19.
[8] *Ibid.*, p. 44.

cities and kingdoms remain consistent throughout the juvenile manuscripts and events are set against what becomes a familiar background.

Branwell soon provided Glass Town with its own miniature journal, "Branwells Blackwoods Magazine." Like many of the children's early writings, this was modeled on *Blackwood's Edinburgh Magazine*. Mr. Brontë's own works also provided stimulus and example for his children's tiny hand-sewn booklets.[9] His love of literature and the fact that he had published several small volumes were early incentives to the young writers. The Brontës had free access to their father's library, which contained many precedents for the tiny books which they produced. The small size of "Something about Arthur" (9.2 × 5.6 cm) is not so unusual as it may seem. Charlotte's own copy of *Paradise Lost*, for example, and her *Le Nouveau Testament De Notre Seigneur Jesus-Christ*,[10] which she received as a school prize on 14 December 1831, are almost the same size as "Something about Arthur."

While the smallness of the early manuscripts and Charlotte's microscopic writing were dictated by the size of the toy soldiers for whom the Glass Town literature was originally written, other factors probably contributed: the cost and scarcity of paper at Haworth, and the inconvenience of the four-mile journey to the nearest stationers at Keighley; a desire to hide writings from adult eyes; and, most significantly, Charlotte's attempt to imitate newspaper and magazine print. There is evidence that Mr. Brontë knew of his children's cramped writing and disapproved: in 1833 he wrote inside one of Charlotte's notebooks, "All that is written in this book, must be in a good, plain and legible hand.   P.B."[11]

In August 1829, Charlotte took over the production of the magazine and changed the name to "Blackwoods Young Mens Magazine." Although she still worked closely with Branwell, who occasionally contributed material, the magazine increasingly became a vehicle for the expression of her own interests and creativity. Charlotte wrote reviews, dialogues, poems, and stories for and about the developing Glass Town society. Sometimes she wrote as editor, sometimes as Captain Tree, her earliest pseudonym. Rapidly Glass Town produced authors, artists, poets, and critics whose voices the young authors could assume. By August 1830,

---

[9] Cf. the title page of Charlotte's unpublished story "The Adventures Of Mon Edouard de Crack" with that of Mr. Brontë's "The Cottage in the Wood," in *Brontëana: The Rev. Patrick Brontë's Collected Works*, ed. J. Horsfell Turner (Bingley, 1898), p. 101.

[10] Brontë Parsonage Museum collection: nos. 29 and 131 respectively.

[11] British Library manuscript: Ashley 170.

when Charlotte began the second series of the magazine, the chief contributors were the Duke of Wellington's two sons: Arthur, Marquis of Douro, and Lord Charles Wellesley, the hero and the author respectively of "Something about Arthur." Most of Charlotte's early poems were written under the pseudonym of "Marquis of Douro." He became a leading Glass Town poet with a penchant for romantic themes, while his younger brother preferred to write prose and drama. Captain Tree continued to contribute occasional articles to the "Young Mens Magazine," as the second series was called, but his role was gradually usurped by his young rival, Lord Charles Wellesley.

The second dreamworld, "Our Fellows," was shortlived and was replaced within six months of its creation by that of "The Islanders."[12] It was "The Islanders," the third and last of the Brontë children's "Plays," which had the greatest influence on Charlotte's early creative writing. While Branwell was still occupied with "Branwells Blackwoods Magazine" for the Young Men, Charlotte wrote her first volume of "Tales of the Islanders." Like the two previous plays, it began with the choosing of chief men and the kingdoms they were to inhabit, in this case famous contemporaries and islands off the coast of Britain. In 1829, Charlotte described the formation of this play:

> Branwell chose the Isle of Man, Emily Isle of Arran and Bute Isle, Ane Jersey and I chose the Isle of Whight. we then chose who should live in our Islands. the chief of Branwell's where Jhon Bull, Astly Cooper, Leigh Hunt &, Emily's Walter Scott, Mr. Lockhart, Johny Lockhart & &, Anne's Michal Sadler, Lord Bentick, Henrey Halford & &, and I chose Duke of Wellington & son, North & Co., 30 officers, Mr Abernethy & &.[13]

Although Branwell, Emily, and Anne all participated in "The Islanders," the play was dominated by Charlotte. "Tales of the Islanders" deals

---

[12] Established in July 1827, "Our Fellows" is referred to in only three manuscripts: in "The History of the Year" and in "The origin of the O'Deans," both written by Charlotte in 1829; and in Branwell's "History of the Rebellion in My Fellows" (incorrectly listed in bibliographies as "History of the Rebellion in My Army"), written in 1828. By December 1827 "Our Fellows" had already given place to "The Islanders."

[13] "The origin of the Islanders," 12 March 1829; unpublished manuscript bound in at the beginning of "Tales of the Islanders": New York Public Library, Berg Collection. Charlotte rewrote this account three months later, on 30 June 1829, in "Tales of the Islanders," vol. 1. Publications of this later account have been inaccurately transcribed and confused with the earlier description: see *The Life of Charlotte Brontë*, vol. 1, pp. 91–3, and Winifred Gérin, *Charlotte Brontë: The Evolution of Genius* (Oxford: Clarendon, 1967), p. 31. I have supplied punctuation in my excerpt but have preserved Charlotte's spelling.

almost exclusively with the adventures of her particular characters. Furthermore, she developed the play from her own point of view, and the action of almost all the tales centers on her hero, the Duke of Wellington. In the play, geographical realism evolves into "a beautiful fiction" known as Vision Island.

Since January 1828, when the real Duke of Wellington had become Prime Minister of England, the Brontë children had followed his career in such newspapers as the *Leeds Intelligencer* and the *Leeds Mercury*. As a result, "Tales of the Islanders" is based on political events. For example, in Volume I, Chapter 3, Charlotte, influenced by her Tory father and by Whig criticism of Wellington in the *Mercury*, describes an attempt by Ratten, the imaginary son of the *Mercury*'s Whig editor, to poison the Duke, whom he accuses of obscuring "the bright dawn of Whigish intellect!" Furthermore, the young Brontës's intense interest in the Catholic Emancipation Bill of 1829 and their subsequent neglect of the Palace School led to "The School Rebellion" in Volume II. The schoolchildren, who had been "becoming something like civilized beings," suddenly degenerate, splitting into four factions based on the political sympathies of the time. Eventually the Duke arrives in a balloon from "Strathfieldsaye," his country estate, to quell the rebellion with a single autocratic threat. Charlotte is reflecting here the Brontë family admiration for the Duke of Wellington's handling of the Catholic Emancipation Bill, despite contemporary doubts and opposition.[14] In the play, when the Brontë children become tired of the Palace School, they send the pupils home so that "only fairys dwell in the Island of dream."

As late as 30 June 1830, Charlotte was writing adventure stories for her fourth volume of "Tales of the Islanders." In *The Brontës' Web of Childhood*, published in 1941, Fannie Elizabeth Ratchford states that "From the play of the Islanders the little Brontës turned again to the wooden soldiers and the Young Men's Play" (p. 11). An examination of the sequence of Charlotte's manuscripts, however, shows that the creative process is not so simple as this. For a year and a half the "Young Men's Play" and "The Islanders" continued to develop side by side. Many elements, especially

---

[14] Both Wellington and Mr. Brontë were born in Ireland, and although Tories of Protestant stock and opposed to what Charlotte calls "Romish Religion " they championed the rights of Ireland. "Tales of the Islanders" vol. 2, chap. 4, shows that Charlotte saw Wellington as the "saviour" of an Ireland oppressed more by Catholic "bigotry" than by Union with Britain. She also records that Aunt Branwell thought the Catholic Emancipation Bill was "excellent" and that the Catholics could "do no harm with such good security."

the principal characters, overlapped. Gradually the plays merged into a single imaginary vision. By the end of 1830, Charlotte's last year at home before entering boarding school, the main elements of "The Islanders" and "Young Men's Play" had become what I term "The Glass Town Saga."

Charlotte remained at Roe Head school for fifteen months, leaving in May 1832. (She was to return to Roe Head in July 1835 as an assistant teacher.) A conscientious pupil, Charlotte had felt keenly "that she was an object of expense to those at home"[15] and as a result she had had neither the time nor the inclination to continue the prolific writing of previous years. Yet her imaginary world continued to haunt her. She was homesick and found relief in daydreams. Her schoolfriend Mary Taylor later told Mrs. Gaskell that Charlotte's "habit of 'making out' interests" for herself "that most children get who have none in actual life, was very strong in her. The whole family used to 'make out' histories, and invent characters and events. I told her sometimes they were like growing potatoes in a cellar. She said, sadly, 'Yes! I know we are!' "[16] Charlotte must have thought often about Glass Town and the inhabitants of her African kingdom, for her writing during the school holidays testifies to this continued interest. But it was only when she finally left school that the intense literary activity of the years 1829 and 1830 was resumed.

"SOMETHING ABOUT ARTHUR" AND THE LATER JUVENILE MANUSCRIPTS

"Something about Arthur" is dated 1 May 1833, one year after Charlotte finished her studies at Roe Head. Many of the characters and scenes were drawn from the early plays, but her one-and-a-half years away from home had given her increased confidence in her writing, new material to draw on, and the ambition to try longer works.

Charlotte's awareness of political events had been sharpened by her recent experiences at Roe Head. As in "Tales of the Islanders," she crudely

---

[15] Ellen Nussey, "Reminiscences of Charlotte Brontë," reprinted from *Scribner's Monthly*, May 1871, *Brontë Society Transactions*, vol. 2, part 10 (1899): 62–3.
[16] *The Life of Charlotte Brontë*, vol. 1, p. 116.

mirrored these events in her stories. The 1830s were years of industrial upheaval in Britain, and Roe Head was situated in the center of the West Yorkshire clothweaving industry. Here she would have learned from Miss Wooler her headmistress, and from others, of earlier industrial unrest caused by the replacement of laborers by machinery, and particularly of the 11 April 1812 attack on Rawfolds Mill in Liversedge by desperate clothworkers armed with pistols, hatchets, and bludgeons. Mrs. Gaskell tells how the owner, Mr. Cartwright, successfully defended the mill but how, soon after, another manufacturer was shot.[17] Mr. Brontë had also lived in this area during these Luddite riots and would have told his children stories of such perilous times.

These well-established sources for the mill attack in *Shirley* may be the source of the similar episode presented here in "Something about Arthur." The silent march of the workers, armed with crude weapons, towards one of "those vile rumbling mills," as well as the workers's attitude towards the "incessant crash of its internal machinery" and towards its master, are reminiscent of the attack on Rawfolds and crudely foreshadow the raid on Robert Moore's mill in *Shirley*.

"The Bridal," a poem and story written immediately after Charlotte's return from Roe Head, bears an even closer relationship to times of industrial unrest. Here Charlotte refers to the Great Rebellion in the Glass Town Federation, recently initiated by Branwell in "Letters from an Englishman," Volume III (11 July 1831). For Branwell, the rebellion is still essentially a game of war between toy soldiers, but Charlotte uses it to show her new awareness of social reality. Her wedding story is interrupted to include this incongruous description, too close in content to the period of the Luddite riots for that association to be ignored:

> Unequivocal symptoms of dissatisfaction began to appear at the same time among the lower orders in Verdopolis. The workmen at the principal mills and furnaces struck for an advance of wages, and, the masters refusing to comply with their exorbitant demands, they all turned out simultaneously. Shortly after, Colonel Grenville, one of the great millowners, was shot .... The police were now doubled. Bands of soldiers were stationed in the more suspicious parts of the city, and orders were issued that no citizen should walk abroad unarmed. In this state of affairs Parliament was summoned to consult on the best measures to be taken.[18]

[17] *The Life of Charlotte Brontë*, vol. 1, pp. 120-23. See also Herbert J. Rosengarten, "Charlote Brontë's *Shirley* and the *Leeds Mercury*," *Studies in English Literature*, vol. 16, no. 4 (Autumn, 1976), pp. 593-600.

[18] *Miscellaneous and Unpublished Writings*, vol. 1, pp. 210-11.

"Something about Arthur" shows a marked advance in the handling of this new material. Dissatisfaction among the lower orders of society no longer intrudes upon a love story, as it did in "The Bridal," but performs a functional role in the plot. It is because of Arthur's involvement with the insurrection that he meets and falls in love with Mina Laury. The "rare lads" or lower-class Verdopolitans, intent on burning Lord Caversham's mill, are no longer purposeless thugs: they are insurgents committed to a social cause. Charlotte is learning to select and transpose her historical facts. "Something about Arthur" shows a new sense of literary freedom.

Current affairs reported in the local newspapers continued to be a major source of material for the juvenilia. For example, references in "Something about Arthur" to the release of millworkers from slavery may owe their origin to Charlotte's knowledge of the abolition of slavery in 1833, the year in which this manuscript was written. Although the Emancipation Act was not passed until 28 August, the issue was much in the public eye in the preceding months. The reference to police in this manuscript was also topical. The Metropolitan Police force was established in England by Robert Peel in 1829, four years before Charlotte wrote "Something about Arthur." Peel was Wellington's Home Secretary and Charlotte had already used him as a character in "Tales of the Islanders," where she refers to his inheritance of a baronetcy in May 1830.

After her return from school, Charlotte's writing was also strongly influenced by the historical novels of Sir Walter Scott. She had long been familiar with his work. In 1828 the four Brontë children were given Scott's *Tales of a Grandfather* by their Aunt Branwell, and Mr. Brontë had owned a copy of *The Lay of the Last Minstrel* since his university days. Faint pencil script and scribbled faces inside the covers of the latter book show that it was well used by the young Brontës.[19] Sir Walter Scott had been one of Emily's chief characters in "The Islanders" play and Charlotte's early poetry contains occasional echoes of Scott. Only now, however, did her writing become pervaded by a sense of medieval romance.

The poem of "The Bridal," for instance, describes the marriage of Arthur to Marian Hume in terms of a medieval feast. Wine "Gleamed in

---

[19] Walter Scott, *The Lay of The Last Minstrel* (London, 1806), Brontë Parsonage Museum: no. 213; inscribed "P Bronte BA St Johns College, Cambridge."

the wine-cup and wassail-bowl" and guests danced to the music "of viol and lute":

> Now white robes fluttered and tall plumes glanced
> While nobles and ladies in bright rings danced,
> Gracefully gliding the pillars among
> To the sound of the harps and the joyous song.

The courtship is even more reminiscent of the world of romance:

> The young knight made a solemn vow
>   Of constancy till death;
> Truth's light beamed on his marble brow
>   While he pledged his knightly faith.[20]

In "Something about Arthur," written after "The Bridal," the narrator, Lord Charles Wellesley, imitates Scott's narrative method and moves from the immediate past to a more distant past in the life of the Marquis of Douro, so presenting a more sophisticated time structure than the mere narration of contemporary events. Lord Charles ignores his brother's recent marriage to Marian Hume until the final page of the story, and records instead an earlier love affair in the life of Arthur, Marquis of Douro. The more obvious references to medieval romance have departed, although Arthur's uncompromising code of honor owes its example to tales of knightly chivalry: he asserts that "a life stained by dishonour is but a protracted species of death."

On 1 January 1833, the seventeen-year-old Charlotte wrote to Ellen Nussey, her closest school friend:

> I am glad you like 'Kenilworth'; it is certainly a splendid production, more resembling a Romance than a Novel, and in my opinion one of the most interesting works that ever emanated from the great Sir Walter's pen .... [Varney] is certainly the personification of consummate villainy, and in the delineation of his dark and profoundly artful mind, Scott exhibits a wonderful knowledge of human nature....[21]

The influence of *Kenilworth* is strongly felt in Charlotte's manuscripts immediately following "Something about Arthur." Fannie E. Ratchford was the first to recognize Scott's influence on Charlotte's writing, although

---

[20] *Miscellaneous and Unpublished Writings*, vol. 1 pp. 203–4.
[21] Thomas James Wise and John Alexander Symington, eds., *The Brontës: Their Lives, Friendships and Correspondence* [The Shakespeare Head Brontë], (Oxford: Basil Blackwell, 1932), vol. 1, p. 109.

she stressed the similarity of *Ivanhoe* rather than *Kenilworth* to Charlotte's story of "The Green Dwarf."[22] Elements in the plot of *Kenilworth* —the secret marriage between Amy Robsart and the Earl of Leicester, the "consummate villainy" of Varney, the faithful admirer Tressilian, the heroine's exile attended by an older man and his daughter, and Amy's eventual death—are echoed throughout the manuscripts of 1833 and 1834 as Charlotte describes the lives of her Verdopolitan characters. "The Green Dwarf   A Tale Of The Perfect Tense" (2 September 1833) tells of the abduction of a heroine and the machinations of a "dark and profoundly artful mind," that of Alexander Percy (originally "Rogue," favorite creation of Branwell, but later the great Earl of Northangerland, political rival and father-in-law, by a second marriage, to Arthur). In "The Secret" (November 1833), Marian Hume is accused of a secret earlier marriage and is aided in her efforts to prove her innocence by Ned Laury and his daughter Mina. The marriage of John of Fidena in "Lily Hart" (7 November 1833) must for many years remain a secret from his father Alexander Sneaky, King of Sneaky's Land. This same John of Fidena was always an admirer of Marian Hume. We learn in her "Last Will and Testament" (5 January 1834) and in "A Peep Into A Picture Book" (30 May 1834) of his enduring friendship and kindness to her when she is deserted by Arthur. Again, in "High Life In Verdopolis" (20 February–20 March 1834), we find Mina Laury, like Marian Hume and Amy Robsart before her, forced by circumstances to live in the seclusion of a country manor house.

Such brief references as those above indicate not only the influence on Charlotte's writing of her recent experience and reading but the fact that "Something about Arthur" is just one strand of a closely woven web of stories and poems. Each of the juvenile manuscripts shows a further development in plot. Settings and characters continually undergo change, and "Something about Arthur," like the other manuscripts, records these developments in Charlotte's writing.

By the time "Something about Arthur" was written, Verdopolis had grown into a commercial center: a "gigantic emporium of commerce, of arts, of God-like wisdom, of boundless learning, and of superhuman knowledge."[23] The old aura of magic and splendor still hovers above it, though the Genii have gone. The city sits "like a queen upon the waters."

---

[22] Fannie E. Ratchford and William Clyde DeVane, eds., *Legends of Angria* (New Haven: Yale University Press, 1933), pp. 1–2.

[23] *Miscellaneous and Unpublished Writings*, vol. 1, p. 205.

Its architecture is of the most noble kind, based on "pure classic taste" and symmetry. The distinguishing landmarks of Verdopolis are the great Tower-of-All-Nations (based on the biblical Tower of Babel), the Hall of Justice, St. Michael's Cathedral, Waterloo Palace, the Grand Inn (or Bravey's Hotel), the Great Square and the Great Bridge spanning the River Guadima, whose banks are decked with prosperous mills and warehouses. The city is continually expanding up the wide fertile Verdopolitan Valley and its harbor is crowded with ships from many nations.

Verdopolis and its province are ruled on a parliamentary system by all four kings of the Glass Town Federation: the Duke of Wellington, Alexander Sneaky, Sir William Edward Parry, and Captain John Ross. Crashie, who presides over the Grand Verdopolitan Horserace in "Something about Arthur," was the original leader of the twelve wooden soldiers in the "Young Men's Play." He has now assumed a semidivine position as "the mighty & venerable patriarch," revered by all for his great wisdom.[24] Verdopolitan society consists mainly of aristocrats, merchants (including visiting Englishmen), and "rare lads" or "rare apes," who form the mass of the lower classes from which the notorious Glass Town villains emerge. Englishmen, who visit the African kingdom for purposes of trade, are always amazed at the splendor of the new country. They are easily distinguished from its inhabitants, however, by their consumptive appearance, and are treated with suspicion and ridicule.[25]

Lord Charles Wellesley is now Charlotte's established mouthpiece. The only exception to this in the years 1832-1835 is "The Foundling. A Tale Of Our Times," written by Captain Tree. As we see in "Something about Arthur," Lord Charles is a fluent narrator; his conversation is witty and full of literary, biblical, and classical allusions. Yet as a character he is inconsistent. Precocious and worldly-wise in his attitude towards his audience, he is a mere child in his relationship with other characters. He is still a very early sketch of the more mature Charles Townshend (Charlotte's mouthpiece of the later juvenilia) or, indeed, of William Crimsworth in *The Professor*.

After Charlotte's return from Roe Head, Arthur, Marquis of Douro, becomes the focus of her writing. He is still an elegant young man, well-versed in literature and science, a champion sportsman and a connoisseur of art, and his new bride, Marian Hume, is still the fairy-tale princess of

---

[24] *Miscellaneous and Unpublished Writings* vol. 1, pp. 77-79 and 282-3.
[25] See *Something about Arthur*, p. 49, and Branwell's "Letter from an Englishman," *Miscellaneous and Unpublished Writings*, vol. 1, pp. 97-158.

the earlier manuscripts, dressed always in green and white and "infinitely too beautiful for this earth."[26] Here, in "Something about Arthur," however, Charlotte now adds to the picture of her hero two complicating factors: a petulant stubbornness and an early love affair. Her knowledge of human nature had been enlarged by her reading and her experience at Roe Head. Her once perfect hero is perfect no longer. In the later juvenilia, as Charlotte falls increasingly under the influence of Byron rather than of Scott, she develops a demonic side to Arthur's nature. He remains the darling of cultured society, surrounded by an adoring circle of females, but he becomes callous in his attitude towards women and ruthless in his pursuit of ambition. In "Something about Arthur" we see the adolescent Douro and witness the first of his many *affaires*.

Mina Laury, who appears for the first time in "Something about Arthur," is to be the oldest and most faithful of Arthur's mistresses. Her peasant background is often referred to in the later juvenilia but until now her early relationship with the Marquis of Douro has been a mystery. With the publication of this story we are able to understand the often cryptic references to her in later manuscripts. At the beginning of "The Spell," for example, we learn of the death of Arthur's son by Marian Hume, despite the efforts of his nurse Mina Laury, "whose tenderness once raised the father but could not raise the son to life." In "Something about Arthur," Charlotte describes Mina's care of "the father" and traces in detail the early innocent romance between the "proud, Aristocratic, high-minded, refined, elegant Marquis of Douro" and the "poor low-born Peasant's Daughter," which is later to provide her with material for an illicit relationship.

Ned Laury, Mina's father, and his "rare lads" are an established element of Glass Town society by 1833. Ned was introduced by Branwell in "Letters from an Englishman," Volume I (6 September 1830), as a huge man, "ferocious and weatherbeaten,"[27] an accomplished poacher and member of Dr. Hume Badey's grave-robbing gang. In "Something about Arthur," however, Ned becomes more than a caricature. He emerges as a loyal retainer and as a father figure, in contrast to the cold, forbidding Duke of Wellington.

Ned Laury and his lower-class compatriots illustrate developments in Charlotte's style, especially her increasing experimentation with language.

[26] *Miscellaneous and Unpublished Writings*, vol. 1, p. 206.
[27] *Ibid.*, p. 101. There is a brief earlier reference to him in the "Advertisements" of "Blackwoods Young Mens Magazine" for September 1829.

Their racy dialogue (an example is Ned's phrase "a soda sick sucking-pig") betrays the young Brontës's fondness for the low life of pot-houses and taverns, encountered first in "Noctes Ambrosianae" in *Blackwood's Edinburgh Magazine* and then transposed into the "Young Mens Magazine" as "Nights," a series of conversations held in Bravey's Hotel. Language is now used by Charlotte as an indication of class. Ned's indignation at the shooting of Thunderbolt ("In the name of my mother's night-cap what did you do that for?") contrasts strongly with the Marquis's rather pompous reply. Lieutenant Tree's speech in "Something about Arthur" represents one of Charlotte's earliest attempts to reproduce a regional dialect,[28] and Arthur's formal speech to his band of followers is a new realistic narrative device in Charlotte's writing at this time. This device occurs first in "The Bridal" and then recurs throughout the stories of 1832-1835, often forming a complete manuscript such as the "Speech of His Grace The Duke of Zamorna At the Opening of the First Angrian Parliament" (20 September 1834).

The frequent biblical and classical references in "Something about Arthur" can be traced to Charlotte's earliest writing, and although they occur here as isolated allusions with little symbolic effect, they show an early use of the rich allusive language of *Jane Eyre* and the later novels. Charlotte probably borrowed many classical phrases from her brother Branwell, who was taught Greek and Latin by his father at this time and whose early manuscripts abound in Homeric allusions.

Branwell influenced much of Charlotte's early writing, and it is interesting to note the similarity of phrases used by brother and sister during this period, an indication of their close cooperation. Charlotte's portrait of Captain Tree in this story, for example, with his "little cocked nose" glowing "like a ruby of the first water" as he sits embracing a bottle of Potheen and uttering "such eldritch screams of laughter as might have appalled the stoutest heart," echoes the language of Branwell's "The Monthly Intelligencer" written several months earlier: Lord Charles, having pricked Captain Tree in the leg with an immense pin, chases him about the dining room "uttering peals of eldritch laughter."[29] The swaggering vocabulary of drunkards can also be traced to Branwell's writing, and the Bacchanalian song in "Something about Arthur" is no surprise to a student of the early juvenilia.

[28] See also "A Day at Parry's Palace," in the "Young Mens Magazine" for October 1830.
[29] *Miscellaneous and Unpublished Writings*, vol. 1, p. 187.

"Something about Arthur" also shows an advance in Charlotte's use of the dramatic. She makes an effort, however crude, to conclude Chapters 3 and 4 with a climax and so tries to create a sense of suspense. The reader's impression of this early story, however, is one of over-dramatic violence. This element of melodrama is possibly a vestige of the childhood plays which were originally acted rather than written. Moreover, Ellen Nussey recalled that strange tales of horror and violence were commonplace in the Brontë home at this time. She noted in her "Reminiscences of Charlotte Brontë" that Mr. Brontë used to relate "stories which made one shiver and shrink from hearing; but they were full of grim humor and interest to Mr. Brontë and his children."[30] It is natural that elements of these stories would appear in the juvenilia, which even so are remarkable for their lack of a sense of horror. Characters seldom suffer realistically or die a permanent death; they are often killed for narrative purposes in one story, but resurrected in the next.

After the composition of "Something about Arthur," Charlotte was to continue her literary apprenticeship for another seven years. But her center of interest gradually changed from Verdopolis to Adrianopolis, a city to the northeast of the original Glass Town.[31] Here Arthur, now Duke of Zamorna, established a new kingdom of Angria and gathered round him a rising generation of men and women, new material for the eager young novelist's pen. Until the age of twenty-four, Charlotte continued to write stories about her imaginary world, its characters, its scenery, and its rivalries in love and war.

"Something about Arthur" looks forward to the later juvenilia in which Arthur is constantly engaged in warfare, especially in winning and defending his new kingdom. As he tells Ned, his expedition in "Something about Arthur" is his "first essay in the art of war but mind what I say Ned, it shall not be my last."

The truancy of Lord Charles Wellesley, mentioned in the opening chapters and underlined by the parallel plot of a similar incident in the life of his elder brother, is an instance of Charlotte's preoccupation with the theme of two rival brothers, so explicitly explored at the beginning of *The Professor*. Edward and William Crimsworth have their more obvious precursors in the later juvenilia (in Edward and William Percy), but the

---

[30] *Brontë Society Transactions*, vol. 2, part 10 (1899): 79.

[31] See "My Angria and the Angrians," *Miscellaneous and Unpublished Writings*, vol. 2, pp. 1–49.

well-known contrast between the real Duke of Wellington's sons provided Charlotte with early material for this theme. Lord Charles's attitude towards his elder brother's condescension and his reference to the parable of the Prodigal Son in "Something about Arthur" mark the antagonism between the two brothers.

The conventional romantic theme in "Something about Arthur" is also continued throughout the juvenile manuscripts. It is closely associated with Charlotte's acute consciousness of class. To Mina, the peasant's daughter, Arthur appears "in the light of a superior being." To marry her he must renounce friends, rank, and wealth, an idea not to be countenanced by the Duke, who in his usual *deus-ex-machina* role abruptly curtails this "childish affair." Mina's position in later manuscripts, however, as Arthur's devoted mistress, appears to be totally acceptable to the young author. The possibilities of moral fortitude and the plea against the injustice of accidental birth, found in the presentation of Elizabeth Hastings in the later juvenilia and then in the heroine of *Jane Eyre*, have not yet presented themselves.

The later manuscripts of 1836–1838 portray Mina as Arthur's most constant mistress. She becomes the Claire Claremont of a now Byronic Hero, following him into exile when civil war and invasion ravage his new kingdom of Angria.[32] In Canto I of "Zamorna's Exile" (19 July 1836) we see the early Mina of "Something about Arthur" and what she has since become:

> Beautiful creature, once so innocent,
>   With such a seriousness and strength of mind
> Beaming upon her youthful brow and blent
>   With what seemed like religion, so refined,
> So firm in principle! Her soul ne'er bent
>   Nor wavered midst the soft voluptuous wind
> A Western palace round the wild rose blew,
> But shook not from it one pure drop of dew.
>
> What is she now? Look at her as the flashing
>   Of her dark Italian eye shines full on me;
> Look at the little hand so proudly dashing
>   The gloomy rain that will stream fitfully
> From the full sphere, her cheek of roses washing
>   Till even its bright bloom fades, and we may see

---

[32] See Winifred Gérin, ed., *Five Novelettes* (London: Folio Press, 1971), p. 125.

> Traces of sorrow there, lit up the while
> With that lost, fated, God-abandoned smile.[33]

When in "Mina Laury" (17 January 1838) Lord Hartford offers her marriage, Mina is powerless to accept: "her very way of life was swallowed up in that of another."[34] She had earlier said in "Passing Events" (29 April 1836), "I've nothing else to exist for, I've no other interest in life."[35] Her continual references to Arthur as "my master" clearly express her predicament and foreshadow Jane Eyre's references to Rochester. Jane Eyre's passionate cry, "My future husband was becoming to me my whole world; and, more than the world: almost my hope of heaven,"[36] has its obvious origin in the juvenilia. Yet Mina Laury and even Elizabeth Hastings are only crude studies for the later Jane Eyre. Charlotte still had much to learn, as she admitted in the Preface to her first novel, *The Professor*; but it was through juvenile works such as "Something about Arthur" that she had the opportunity to develop the powerful elements of her later writing.

THE TEXT

The text presented here follows as closely as possible Charlotte's original manuscript. Her idiosyncrasies of spelling, punctuation, and capitalization have been preserved in the transcription, and her deletions and corresponding corrections in the manuscript have been listed at the end of this edition. The list includes a few words which occur in the middle of or next to a deletion and which obviously were supposed to have been deleted. Charlotte usually wrote additions or corrections to her manuscript above the relevant line and indicated their correct position by a caret. Her additions which do not replace a deleted word or phrase are included in the text but no attempt is made to indicate their position. Her hyphenation, except where it occurs at the end of a line, is preserved. Editorial insertions are made in square brackets, where the addition of a letter or

---

[33] *Legends of Angria*, pp. 126–7.
[34] *Five Novelettes*, p. 165.
[35] *Ibid.*, p. 44.
[36] Jane Jack and Margaret Smith, eds., *Jane Eyre* (Oxford: Clarendon, 1969), p. 346.

word has been thought necessary to convey the sense. In her early writings, Charlotte abbreviated proper names by simply using initial letters. Where this occurs in "Something about Arthur" the remainder of the name is supplied in square brackets. Doubtful readings are indicated in a square bracket with a question mark. Occasionally, when a word has run off the page at the end of a line, the missing letter has been silently supplied. The original line-endings are not indicated in this transcription.

Charlotte's punctuation is particularly haphazard, and sentence endings in the manuscript are often left unmarked. She had not yet begun to use the dashes, so frequent in her later manuscripts, to indicate a comma or full stop. In the transcription, punctuation has been added or altered where necessary to facilitate reading. The added punctuation is printed in semi-bold type. Editorial alterations in punctuation together with such emendations as the elision of words unnecessarily repeated in the manuscript are listed at the back of this edition. The explanatory notes to the text include descriptions of some of the terms and minor characters in "Something about Arthur." A list at the end provides the dates and sources of manuscripts referred to in this edition.

The original manuscript consists of thirteen leaves, each approximately 9.2 × 5.6 cm. The text begins on the recto of the first leaf and continues on both sides of each leaf, concluding on the recto of the thirteenth. A solidus (/) is used in this transcription to mark the end of each manuscript page. Charlotte wrote the pages separately, and then sewed them together inside a brown paper sheet of the same size in order to make a small booklet. This is typical of almost all her early manuscripts. The title, signature, and date appear at the end of the manuscript; however, in this transcription, the title has been transposed to the beginning of the text.

Charlotte's later manuscripts, written on loose sheets of paper, give the impression of hasty composition: the lineation is often crooked, for she sometimes wrote with her eyes shut in an effort to preserve the image she was describing. "Something about Arthur," however, shows considerable care in production; the small handmade booklet was intended as a final copy and not as an early draft. Occasionally words are repeated—an indication of hesitancy rather than speed. The minute script is carefully formed and the lines are straight. Nevertheless, the almost microscopic writing and tiny size of the manuscript made transcription extremely slow and difficult, and the aid of a magnifying glass was often necessary. Charlotte made no attempt at paragraphing, but then the pages of her manuscript are small and the story is divided into six chapters. In order to make the text easier to read, I have introduced paragraph divisions.

The lack of punctuation, surprising in a seventeen-year-old girl, was probably the result of ignorance rather than speed. Charlotte had no early formal education. She was first taught by her father, reared as Mrs. Gaskell says "among the wholesome pasturage of English literature."[37] The register of her first school notes that Charlotte is "Altogether clever of her age, but knows nothing systematically."[38] Miss Wooler, at Roe Head school, also commented on certain deficiencies in Charlotte's previous education and sought to correct them. There is a marked improvement in the punctuation of "The Bridal" and "Something about Arthur" compared to the earliest manuscripts. Miss Wooler, however, was never completely successful and Charlotte was always aware of this; she was later to thank her publishers for re-punctuating *Jane Eyre*, as she "found the task very puzzling."[39] If she had known that "Something about Arthur" was to be published, it seems likely that she would have approved of such regularization of the punctuation as I have attempted.

I would like to express my gratitude to the family of the late Mr. C.K. Shorter for their kind permission to publish this manuscript and particularly to The Brontë Society, whose grant-in-aid made it possible for me to see the original work in Austin, Texas. I should also like to thank my college, Clare Hall, for its financial help; the staff of the Humanities Research Center at The University of Texas at Austin for their generous assistance to me while I was transcribing the manuscript; Dr. Philip Gaskell and Professor Herbert Rosengarten for reading the typescript of this edition; and especially Professor Ian Jack for his constant encouragement and help in my study of Charlotte Brontë's juvenilia.

Christine Alexander

Clare Hall, Cambridge, 1978

---

[37] *The Life of Charlotte Brontë*, vol. 1, p. 60; a quotation from Charles Lamb.

[38] Clergy Daughters' School, Cowan Bridge, recorded 1824: see *The Brontës: Their Lives, Friendships and Correspondence*, vol. 1, p. 69.

[39] 24 September 1847; *The Brontës: Their Lives, Friendships and Correspondence*, vol. 2, p. 142.

Something about Arthur

Written by Charles Albert Florian Wellesley.

A reproduction, to scale, of the first page of the manuscript.

CHAPTER. I

To keep company with those who are far beneath us in rank, or accomplishments whether bodily or mental is the surest method of eradicating those seeds of virtue which parental affection & assiduity may have carefully planted & patiently nourished within us.... Bud.[1]

———

Some months ago, as I was lounging over a book-stall In one of those wretched alleys which intersect Verdopolis, I accidentally drew from a tattered pile of trash an odd volume of Bud's works and on opening it the moral maxim which forms the motto of this chapter met my eye. After reading it over carefully I began to ponder on the connection which I could not deny existed between it and my present circumstances. For upwards of six months I had been a voluntary exile from those higher circles of society with which my birth entitled me to conve[r]se. An unsettled wanderer from one low haunt to another, my precarious subsistence had been derived from the sale of such pathetic balladds and merry tales as my tragic & comic powers (joined to a certain acquaintance with the—feelings & habits of the poor) enabled me to produce. my only companions had been Tavern Keepers, poachers, park-breakers, Highwaymen, Murderers, the flashmen[2] about Town, &c. &c.; my only places of Resort pothouses, the Rendzvous of Robbers & the open fields. With such habits [&] Associates it may easily be imagined that the small stock of knowledge I possessed woould rather be diminished than increased excepting only in what relates to those means & resources with which Vice furnishes us for promoting the misery [&] injury of our fellow-creatures. I had never been slow to learn & accordin[g]ly I quickly adopted the language & manners of my new comrades imitating them to such perfection that they soon declared that I might have been born & bred amongst them. I was proud of their low approbation & every day my efforts to deserve it were renewed. These endeavours were so successful that at the period I speak of little remained to denote my former

31

rank except my shape & complexion, the tone of my voice & my powers of scribbling verses. My shape still retained a certain portion of elegance which the constant excersize I took rather added to than lessened. My complexion despite of incessant exposure to all weathers continued tolerably fair. Nature having given me a not disagreeable voice, I could no[t] if I would have rendered it otherwise. As for my Ryhming propensities, since they contributed to my support I did not / feel inclined to discard them.

Such was the state of things when by a curious coincidence my eye happened to glance on Buds' moral observation. circumstances of apparently trifling importance sometimes awaken men's consciences when loud & solemn warnings have repeatedly failed. These few lines raised a crowd of Remorseful feelings for the mad unthinking manner in which I had relinquished the elegant delights of cultivated society, the benefits of a liberal education, the pleasures of rational conversation & last [but] not least the splendid luxuries of an affluent home. For gentle reader if the Truth must be spoken (& I may as well make a clean breast of it while I am engaged in the work of confession) two of the principal circumstances which led me in to this gloomy but salutary train of thought, were that my only pillow that night had been the curb stone of the cause-way & my only breakfast in the morning a mouthful of cold raw air from the river and Now my Aching Head, my empty stomach, my Rag-covered back & my bare & bleeding feet were In my mind as so many powerful casuists each bringing forward unanswerable arguments to prove that it was my duty to reform & return like the Repentant Prodigal[3] to my father's house where my heart told me I was sure of finding a hearty unreproachful welcome from every inmate of those still dear though forsaken walls. At first I made a feeble resistance to their close & cogent reasoning but the keen cravings of Hunger rapidly thawed any slight objections. bright visions began to dawn on my now excited imagination in which the cook armed with spit, frying-pan & gridiron appeared as a prominent figure. their pathetic pleading compleatly overcame & girding up my loins for the journey which was full three miles from the place where I then was I set off strengthened by the expectation of the good cheer which I knew woould await me on my arrival at the conclusion. /

CHAP. II

I reached Waterloo-Palace[4] in a half famished condition but the cordial reception I met with quickly restored by almost exhausted spirits. After receiving my dear Father's embrace & blessing & satisfying the pressing demands of a perfectly ravenous appetite I retired to rest for it was now late in the evening. The whole night I had but one nap for the now unwonted luxury of a down bed & rose-scented sheets of the finest cambric wrapped me in such a paridisaical repose as can only be purchased at the price of severe previous hardships. On rising the next morning I proceeded (after repeated ablutions with soap & water) to equip myself in French white silk pantaloons, grass-green vest, mantle & cap (the latter of which was surmounted with two long costly feathers of the bird of Paradise fastened in front by a circular golden ornament set with emeralds) white silk stockings & green morocco sandals. All these articles of dress I found lying on my dressing table together with a perfumed cambric handkerchief and a purse containing several small silver coins. When I had finished dressing and had contemplated myself in the mirror for a reasonable length of time I descended to the breakfast room. My father was alone. he received me with his usual smile & kiss. a[t] these renewed tokens of undiminished affection I felt my heart swelling a little and could not forbear asking him in rather a tremulous tone If he was not displeased at my late disgraceful conduct—"No my darling" said he, "my delight at seeing you return of your own accord with the rose of health restored to the cheek which was before so pale & blanched has quelled every transient feeling of anger which I might have entertained. But Charles, I have permitted your waywardness & caprice full play & now my love I expect you to fall cheerfully into more regular habits." "Father," said I, "your will is my law. you shall now see how I can obey you." he smiled again & patted by head approvingly.

After breakfast I imediately repaired to the sckool-room. I found Mr Rundell[5] already seated at his desk. I suppose he had been apprised of my return as he testified no astonishment when I entred. "Good morning M^r

Rundell," said I with a low bow. "Good morning young gentleman," he returned coldly & stifly. "Your father has charged me to forbear reproach but I must say that if your noble brother had acted when under my authority as you do he would not now be what he is. Of a truth he used sometimes to assume the aspect of a thunder-cloud, to / kick as it were against the pricks & to refuse with a glance of fire and in an attitude of defiance the wholesome chastisement which his occasional restiveness rendered necessary. those I grant were trying times but when I would ask did he ever absent himself for six whole months from his task? Never. When did he ever delight in the company of the low-born & illiterate. Seldom or never." "Indeed Mr Rundell," said I interrupting him, "I fear you have forgotten Arthurs boyish pranks. One frolic of his I should think could never have been erased from your memory. I know you took it sadly to heart at the time." "Silence Sir," exclaimed my Tutor reddening, "And do not recall from oblivion circumstances which ought now to have been utterly forgotten." I felt strongly inclined to throw a saucy answer in his teeth but recollecting that my motto was for the present 'Reform' I checked myself & sat down in silence to my studies. now however I am not under the same restraint & therefore I will by a little anecdote of Arthur's earlier years explain the above passage to my readers.

The affair happened shortly after he had entred his fi[f]teenth year. how well I remember him at this age! so tall and slight with a complexion [? of] effeminate delicacy & transparency, sweet dark eyes & a profusion of brown curling hair. I loved him infinitely better then than I do now and for a very good reason. In those times he thought it no disgrace to favour me with some marks of reciprocal affection. My father then as now was the only person in the world who possessed the slightest authority over him. Of every living thing besides he was, when his frantic moods took him, uttterly disregardful. How often when thwarted & provoked have I seen the crimson blood flushing his fair cheek & a perfect flame of defiance kindling in his eyes & imediately he has assumed a quite calm & dispassionate aspect on my Fathers saying with a smile, "That lad seems possessed by the Great Spirit of Wickedness himself: Come Arthur let me see a little of your self-controul. I'll allow you five minutes to become as cool as I am at this moment." These fits however were only occasional. at other times he was remarkable for his free & affable deportment & his still distinguishing characteristics of Generosity and Gallantry. But I am wandering away from my subject.

about the period above mentioned Arthur became acquainted with a /

young nobleman bearing the name & title of Colonel lord Caversham,[6] a thirsty soul & one who could carry an overdose of wine as reputably as any man in christendom. this capability joined to the accomplishment of being an excellent jockey, dice-caster & card-shuffler formed the whole extent of his attainments. Arthurs admiration of horse-flesh was at this early age almost as ardent as it is now. About this time my Father presented him with a splendid black stallion as full of youthful fire as himself. he thought it the noblest horse in the Universe & regarded it with a delight & affection proportioned to his lofty estimate of its value. He used to frequently clasp its stately neck with both arms and kiss it with rapturous energy again & again while its big veins throbbed & bounded as if they would burst from an overplus of high & vigorous blood. My father often gazed at him with admiration & my mother with trembling as he sat upright as an arow while Thunderbolt,[7] (his charger's name) reared, curvetted, performed the demi-volte & many other equinine feats, & then suddenly burst away with the glancing speed of lightning & bore him in a whirlwind from their sight.

Now it happened that a grand horse-race was to take place at Verdopolis & the prize offered was a statue of the winning horse cast in gold & placed on a pedestal of the same precious metal. Lord Caversham conveyed information of the whole affair to Arthur and hinted in a tone of apparent regret that it was a pity Thunderbolt should not have an opportunity of earning a meed of fame so splendid as that which would undoubtedly accrue to the conqueror. Arthur instantly determined that come what would this glorious opportunity of displaying his favourite's transcendant & peerless excellence should not be lost. he hastend to my father & having imparted the intelligence he had just obtained & preferred a request that Thunderbolt might be permitted to contest the prize he received a cheerful and unhesitating acquiescence in the prayer of his petition.

The Grand day of Experiment at length arrived & at an early hour Arthur repaired burning with irrepressible impatience to the course. he seated himself at a distance from the general crowd of spectators on some steps near the Judges stand. Scarcely did he deign to cast a look at the huge unbroken mass of human faces sloping far above him upwards like a living hill almost to the very clouds. Many of these however were turned with marks of evident astonishment towards the youthful & elegant / figure sitting alone at the bottom of the vast flight of steps which ascended to the throne where the holy & venerable Crashie sat as grand arbiter of the day's proceedings. After a short but anxious interval the horses were brought out and ranged in order. Then the signal for starting was given by a loud flousish of trumpets & a sky-rending cheer from the immense gazing multitude. At once with the speed of light that animated whirlwind swept away. Arthur neither spoke nor stirred as in mute triumph he beheld his own sable steed shoot far a-head of its swift fiery competitors. Already half the race was run and doubtless in imagination he grasped the golden prize & exulted over his less fortunate rivals, When suddenly Thunderbolt stopped & wheeling rapidly round trotted back with great deliberation to the starting post. At this extraordinary manouvre "A shout of unextinguishable laughter"[8] mingled with exclamations of surprise "shook the air". My father who was seated with the other Sovereigns at Crashie's right hand, Glanced anxiously down towards Arthur's station. he remained unchanged in attitued & feature gazing with apparent unconcern at the self-disgraced Charger. In the meantime the victory was hotly contested by the remaining horses but in the end it declared itself in favour of a beautiful bay filly the property of Lord Caversham. Accordingly, the conqueror being led to the foot of the throne by two grooms splendidly attired, Crashie hung a garland of gold-wrought laurel round its neck and having adjudged the prize to George Frederick Baron of Caversham he rose & dissolved the assembly.

In a few hours the thunder of departing crowds died away & by the coming on of twilight Arthur found himself alone with Thunderbolt in the vast area, for he still remained immoveable at his original post. doubtless his mind was occupied with thoughts abstruse and 'tis a great pity I cannot present the result of his meditations to my reader. Perhaps they were on the moon now beginning to shine dimly above him, perhaps on the Western light which was fast fading into darkness; it may be that his brains were a little confused by the dull ceaseless hum of men & waves which rose in a continued mumuring strain over the sloping bounds of the roofless amphitheatre, or perhaps (& this I think is the most probable supposition) he might have been reflecting on the reason which could have induced his charger to turn his back in so contempuous a manner on a prize which to all other eyes seemed worth / striving for.

However this may be, his ideas were soon put to flight by the sound of a footstep close at hand. And looking up he saw the figure of a tall man standing in the moonlight and, as he leant on the glittering stock of a long well-polished fowling peice, regarding him with a pair of keen dark eyes whose expression of earnest curiosity not a little discomposed my very sensitive brother. "What is your object here Sir?" exclaimed Arthur starting to his feet. "Only to know if I can do you a good turn my young chap." "Have you any motive for interesting yourself in my affairs?" "I can't say that I have." "What then induces you to offer me your assistance?" "Why I was present at the race this afternoon and if I'm not mistaken that there losing-horse belongs to you or else you would not stay here alone with it looking so melancholy and concerned on account as I suppose of its comical behaviour." "And if your conjecture is correct what then?" "Why I've a notion that all was not fair play in that affair." "You are right. most certainly there has been some base under-hand dealing. if Thunderbolt had not been wickedly mismanaged, I could stake my life that no horse but one from the infernal regions could possibly outstrip him. I can guess too from what quater the villany proceeded but how to obtain certain information on that head I know not." "There my lad I think I could help you." "How? if you can show me some method of ascertaining whether George Frederick Baron of Caversham is concerned in this transaction or not a rich recompense shall not be lacking." "I see you are a lad of sharpness & spirit. In my mind Caversham has been the main hand in this cheatary and now I'll tell you plainly that if I had not got this crotchet into my head I'd never have stirred the length of a spider's leg to help you. but I've an old grudge against C[aversham], & so it's my delight to give his honnour as much botheration as possible. Now you must know that the jockey who rode your horse is a cousin of mine. a sweet slice of deceit he is as ever wore jerkin or boots, & I've no doubt that if he were properly dosed with what he likes best & pumped by a man of understanding (myself for instance) he'd prudently vomit all up like a soda sick sucking-pig." "Well sir I will leave all that to your judgement & discretion. in the meantime permit me to examine that handsome fowling peice of yours. is it loaded?" "Yes, with ball. here take it but do'nt shoot yourself." Arthur took the weapon & after examin[in]g it for a short time with apparent attention raised it suddenly to his shoulder and taking a careful aim shot Thunderbolt with fatal exactness right through the heart. The noble steed fell heavily to the earth with a deep rattling groan. he rolled his large eyes piteously for a few moments on his murdarer & master then slowly and painfully expired. "In the name of my mother's night-cap what did you do that for?" Exclaimed the owner of the gun gazing at Arthur with an equivocal kind of expression which seemed to say, "I do'nt know whether your brain's cracked or not." "I have my reasons," replied Arthur dashing away the gathering tears from his eyes. "This horse was my pride & glory & I could not have borne to see him live disgraced. a life stained by dishonour is but / a protracted species of death." "but we are going to prove that he was not dishonoured. have you forgotten that my lad?" "No Sir I had not, but you cannot enter into the motives which induced me to perpetrate this apparently barbarous act so I will not detain you by explaining them." "Well the horse is dead so it's no use blabbing about him. Let's begone now or else we shall never do our intents." "I am perfectly ready to depart but first what is your name?" "Ned Laury." "Do you reside in Verdopolis?" "No, I live a long way up the country above a thousand miles off. But once a year I come to pleasure myself to the city. What name am I to give you young'un?" "you may call me 'Arthur.' " "And what besides?" "Nothing." "Nothing, my dainty lad, why you must have a surname." "No I have not." "Then I'll give you one, for on my conscience a rare lad[9] like me would never consent to company with one who can not write his name double like any other christian. You shall be called from this time forward Arthur the white-handed." "Very-well call me what you like." this agreement being concluded they set off, Ned Laury leading the way & Arthur following his guidance.

The moon was beaming with sickly lustre in a sky which though free from clouds presented a hazy & indistinct aspect that added to the low sorrowful sighing of the wind and a dull moaning proceeding from the approximate ocean seemed to portend tempestuous weather. Quickly & quietly they threaded a labyrinth of narrow ruinous lanes whose silence expressively proclaimed the universal dominion of night and sleep. occasionally however bursts of laughter with the softened sound of songs & musical instruments rose apparently from the bowels of the earth. As often as these strange noises "vexed the dull ear of night"[10] Ned Laury exclaimed with an inward chuckle, "Go it my rare apes,[11] I wish I were with you."

At length a louder & more boisterous note of merriment was sounded and at the same instant the red glow of fire-light streamed across their path. It came from the windows of a little low-roofed Pot-house whose sign was a monkey holding in one hand a fair tankard of nut brown ale, the miraculously luxuriant foam of which it quaffed with a visage of most enviable satisfaction. its other forepaw rested on a pile of immense cheeses & its hind legs were supported the one on a brown loaf and the other on a flitch of fat bacon. at the door of this much promising hotel Ned Laury made a halt &, after informing Arthur that it was here he expected to find his cousin, uttered a loud shrill whistle. This summons was immediately answered by the appearance of a gaunt lean figure who issued from an adjoining outhouse, Exclaiming in savage tones, "What does he want a this time of night, he wished he was at the bottom of the sea." "Why you flea's tooth," replied Ned Laury. "What's the matter to night. I've brought you a choice guest & I want to get him into the house & behind the partition of your kitchen without being seen by anyone." / "Let him jump through that window and then follow his nose," returned the uncourteous landlord. "You must do as he desires you," said Ned observing that Arthur hesitated, for his fastidious delicacy revolted a little at the idea of entering so low & mean a place as every-thing denoted this tavern to be. But after a moment's reflection he determined to follow implicitly the directions of his conductor, & accordingly leaping through the small opening pointed out to him, he found himself in a long narrow appartment which seemingly answered the double purpose of a larder and liquour vault, the roof being hung with bacon, salted-beef, dried fish &c., and the floor covered with casks of various forms & dimensions. These arrangements he observed by the light of the moon & that which proceeded from a kind of loop-hole cut in the wooden screen which separated this store-house from the kitchen. "Now my lad," continued Ned, "look through that hole and you'll see & hear every-thing which passes in the next room. before I leave you I must ask one question & that is, who'll provide the stumpy, the blunt,[12] the cash as it were to pay for the liquor that cousin of mine will require before he 'peaches?'" "O make yourself perfectly easy on that head. here is a guinea & if more is wanted I will supply you." "Come there's a smart 'un. you do things like a gentleman. that I must say," and with these words Ned disappeared, the landlord following after having admonished his guest not to steal any of the dainties so tempttingly displayed above & around him.

Arthur now took his station at the loop-hole & commenced his observations. the kitchen which this aperture looked into was a large low roofed appartment illuminated and warmed by an immense blazing fire round which sat on wooden benches eight men who were driving away care with mirth, & songs & ample draughts of the potent Sir John Barleycorn's blood.[13] Seven of these midnight revellers were tall, broad muscular specimens of the Rare Lad Genus with weather-beaten, fear-nought countenances & eyes that twinkled merrily from the combined influence of lighthearts & jovial ale. The eighth was a man of low stature & slender make. the expression of his countenance indicated a disposition to low cunning which a sinister cast in the eyes considerably enhanced. he was attired in a striped jacket with cordurey breeches & jockey-boots.

Scarcely had Arthur taken a cursory view of these chosen associates when the door opened & Ned Laury stalked statelily in. "Well my' lads," said he, "how are ye all?" "We're pretty well off as you may see Ned just now, how we shall be tomorrow-night none of us either knows or cares; but come sit ye down here my rose & take a taste of some saints water." "I do'nt care if I do. Here Landlady," addressing a little bustling Frenchwoman who [performed] the duties of mistress & bar-maid, "a quart of brown stout. Aye Jerry are you here, why whats the matter with you lad. Jerry Sneak I say what ails you. you look quite chop-fallen?" these word[s] were spoken to the small man who certainly did look rather melancholy at / this moment. "Ah cousin Ned," replied he in a whining tone,"I've reason to be chop-fallen. this here tankard is nearly empty & not the smallest coin do I possess to pay for anything more So I must e'en leave this good-company & that too just when you're come to make it better than ever." Here he squeezed some croccodile tears & heaved a deep sigh. "Poor Jerry," said Ned in a tone of pretended sympathy, "How downcast he is. but cheer up lad & you shall share this pot of ale with me." These words produced an instantaneous effect on Jerry. he immediately wiped his eyes & applied himself vigourously to the Tankard.

The song, the joke & the laugh now went round without much intermission. At length conversation began to flag. The company one by one slid softly into the arms of Somnus.[14] Till Ned & Jerry alone remained to continue their noisy vigils. The former now addressed his cousin thus, "Well Jerry they've all left us to sit it out by ourselves. I wish you'd be kind enough to tell me some of your famous exploits on the turf. I daresay you've not passed this day without dishing some flat[15] or other. Now Tell me lad how you contrived to make that horse you rode turn tail so cleverly." "Aye" said Jerry winking, "there-by hangs a tale and as you've treated me so handsomely to-night I dont care if I let you into the whole secret. Now you must know that Lord Caversham sometimes employs me to do little things for him which he has not brains enough to do himself. a few days since he came into my stables while I was cleaning the horses & he says says he [?to me], "Jerry my jewel, I want you to manage a small matter in the jockey line." "I'm quite at your service my Lord," says I. "Well then Jerry," says he, "you must handle that there horse," pointing to a fine black Arab who had been brought to the stables lately. "In such a manner that he will not interfere with my nag on the racecourse next week. You understand me Jerry?" "Aye to be sure my lord," says I, "never fear but I'll contrive the thing to your satisfaction," and so with these words we parted. Well I bothered my poor brains sadly before I could hit on any promising method of tying as it were the black Arab's legs together. At long & last this thought struck me that I might take him every night to the amphitheatre & after riding him to the middle of the cou[r]se trot him slowly back & when he reached the starting post give him a good feed of corn. this scheme answered my highest expectations & tonight Lord Cavers[h]am gave me [?s.o.t.][16] as the reward of my cleverness."

When Jerry had concluded this important comunication, he took a vigourous pull at the tankard which had been just replenished with rum instead of ale. the strength of the draught added to what / he had taken before completely overcame him & he fell back motionless in his seat. Ned payed the reckoning & after recommeneding his cousin to the Land-[l]a[d]y's attentions hastened to discover Arthur in his retreat. On entering the store-room however he found that the bird was already flown but a substantial acknowledgement of Ned's services had been left behind in the shape of a silk purse containing 10 golden guineas. These He immediately took possession of & went away blessing the good fortune which had brought him in contact with a young gentleman of so generous & noble a disposition.

CHAPTER. THE. III

A BALL was this night given by Lady Dunsandle[17] on the occasion of the races at which most of the Elite were present and Lord Caversham among the number. All the company were profuse in their congratulations to him on his happy luck. he was the Lion of the night. Ladies of all ages from the Dowager to the Debutante flocked round him & strove by every method their ingenuity could devise to attract his attention, for Lord Caversham was young and a bachelor possessing a lengthy rent-roll and a not deformed person.

It was now three o'clock. the excitement occasioned by music, dancing, wine, and flattery was just at its height when suddenly the folding-doors were thrown open and a servant announced the Marquis of Douro. Every eye was turned towards him as he entered, he advanced unabashed through the crowd of brilliant guests and bowing gracefully to the Noble Hostess addressed her in these words, "you will doubtless Madam be not a little surprised at the abrupt manner in which I have ventured to intrude uninvited on your prescence. But be assured nothing but the most urgent necessity could have induced me to act thus. I have business of an important nature to transact with one of the present company which cannot be delayed. Lord Caversham is the person to whom I allude." "I," exclaimed his Lordship stepping forward. "What on earth is the matter Arthur?" "If you will retire with me to another appartment I will explain everything to your Lordship privately, but if you are conscious that you have done nothing to be ashamed of the explanation may as well take place were we are." "Ha, Ha, Ha," exclaimed Lord C[aversham], his countenance at the same moment assuming an ashy paleness. "I think thou art somewhat cracked youngster." "Dog," replied Arthur with kindling eyes, "give me a direct answer or (drawing a pistol from his belt) I blow you back to dust." "Impudent young scoundrel!" retorted C[aversham]. "How dare you speak thus to me. Off this instant filthy brat."

The ball-room now became a scene of confusion. ladies were shrieking & swooning in all directions & gentlemen hurridly hastening to their assistance. "You see my lord what disturbance your obstinacy is causing," said Arthur more coolly. "Retire with me or I will directly proclaim your disgrace." L[ord] C[aversham] seeing matters brought [to] this pass thought it was best to consent & accordingly, having summoned one Lieutenant Tree[18] a lick-spittle of his to attend him, he accompanied Arthur into another room. Here in proper terms my brother set forth his mean & treacherous dealing, applied to him a little of that infernal taunting under which he still often makes his opponents writhe, / renounced his friendship forever & concluded by challenging him to singal [combat] with sword or fire-arms as he in his wisdom should judge best. Lord Caversham answered this defiance by a torrent of Billingsgate abuse. He accused Arthur of tampering with his servants, of bribing & pumping his most confidential menials &c. &c. "Come," said Arthur smilling disdainfully, "will you fight or not?" "I fight with thee! thou mongrel whelp, thou lame colt, thou suckling gosling, thou little pale-faced slender girl, no! I'd sooner burn my patent of nobility & sink into a base snob[19] at once." To This tirade of his lordships Tree added, "A must see A think it would be a greet sheeme in your High Loftiness to feaght with any such peice of goods as that young meester." "Hideous Toad," exclaimed Arthur. "You shall suffer for presuming to corrupt the air with your fetid breath," and springing forward he dashed him furiously to the earth & then tied his cravat to such good purpose that the prostrate Lieutenants Life came squirting out in a stream of black blood from his eyes & mouth. Lord C[aversham] perceiving the catastrophe of his favourite contrived to escape by means of a window which opened into the street. Arthur sprung out after him and a regular chase ensued.

On they sped, down Carolus Street, through Palmetto square & down the whole length of the fashionable promenade which adjoins it. Sometimes Arthur gained close on Caversham's heels & sometimes Caversham shot far ahead of his pursuer; panting, puffing & blowing they fled forward as if a legion of evil spirits had been behind. Morning now dawned; the first gleam of rising light struck on the lofty towers of Verdopolis; the first cool Zephyr ruffled the distant sea. They now reached the great central Square. Terror stricken & fainting with fatigue Lord Ca[versham] glanced despairingly round in search of some place of refuge. No resource appeared; the lofty palaces frowning grandly & gloomily on every side stood with barred gates & shuttered windows sternly rejecting his soul-breathed prayer for protection. He looked back & beheld Arthur like a young royal tiger spanging[20] towards him with fearful speed. He looked forward, nothing appeared but the sky-topped monument. He felt a sensation at his heart as if it had been grasped by the cold hand of a corpse; life seemed departing through his lips. A voice shouted in his ear, "wretch I have thee & now I swear by the sun thy blood & liver shall be my meat & drink this day." Roused by this terrible threat, elevated by supernatural dread to supernatural efforts, He sprung to the gigantic pillar, clasped his arms round a portion of the rounded surface & wrigled with serpent swiftness to the very top. Arthur equally excited by rage as he by dread followed his example with the like success. Lord C[aversham], being no longer unmanned by the fearful feeling of pursuit, now recovered strength & courage & A tremendous struggle took place at the height of nine hundred feet above the ground. Each strove to precipitate his adversary to the earth. fire darted from the eyes of the combatants. a livid crimson glowed in their blood streaked visages. with nerves and sinews strained to the very uttermost they wrestled furiously for the space of fifteen minutes. at length the muscular strength of Lord C[aversham] pre- / vailed & whirling rapidly through the void of air, my brother came to the ground with a force that dashed every bone in his body to atoms.

CHAPTER THE IV

Many long months passed away before Arthur recovered from the effects of this memorable encounter. at length the rose of returning health began to bloom on his wan wasted cheek & his enfeebled frame was once more braced with youthful vigour. The desire of Vengeance which had slumbered for a while as he lay writhing with pain & burning with fever in a sick-bed now awoke again in his heart & grew daily as his strength increased.

One evening after sitting alone for some time darkly meditating on the means of gratifying that thirst for revenge which consumed him without arriving at any satisfactory conclusion to his righteous reflections, He took a solitary walk out on the terrace of Waterloo Palace. it was twilight. the evening wind sighed soothingly through the tall trees whose dark boughs shadowed his pathway & mingled its wispers with the sound of distant music & murmuring waves which rose from the Guadiana & the splendid barges that now floated gaily on its heaving bosom. The night was moonless but a dim & fading splendor from the west still faintly illumined every object.

I know not what formed the subject of Arthurs musing as he paced slowly to and fro, but their course was presently broken by the intrusion of [a] Gruff voice exclaiming, "Arthur the white-handed, stop a minute, I want to speak to you." Thus accosted he turned round & beheld Ned Laury standing at one end of the terrace. He advanced towards him with a smile & said, "Well Ned what's your business with me to night? If I can serve you I will." "Why my rare lad I once helped you to get a bit of satisfaction for the dirty turn Lord C[aversham] did you a few months since. I believe the thing did not quite answer your expectations, So I'm come to say that there's another chance for you if you like to take it." "If I like to take it! Why Ned at this moment I'm prepared to move Heaven & Earth for Vengeance." "That's my jewel, you're your father's own son." "But what must I do? tell me & I'll depart this moment." "Do you remember my reason for lending you a lift that time about Thunderbolt?" "I do.

you said Lord C[aversham] had done you some injury." "Yes lad & that injury was He Had taken my old father & clapped him for life into one of those vile rumbling mills of his just for shooting a few brute beasts such as deer & partridges. Now to night I and some other sweet apes are going to burn the mill, kill the Guard & overseers, & let all the prisoners loose. If we succeed it will spite his lordship finely; if not, why we can die like men. Will you go with us or not?" "I will most certainly & doubt not that my heart shall accompany my hand in the business. I must premise this condition: Let me be appointed your leader for I cannot submit to act an under part in any enterprise." "Thats rather bold my lad & would not be granted readily I assure you if we had not before determined this point. but as you are such a genuine chip of[f] the old block we have settled that you shall be our captain to-night." Arthur bowed & without another word they set off.

After two hours walk they reached the place of Rendezvous which was a / retired and shady grove situated on the banks of the Guadiana a few miles out of Town. When they entered it all was silent except the whispering wind & the soft murmurs of the river as it stole gently by. Ned now uttered a shrill whistle. in a few seconds the tramp of footsteps was heard approaching and a glare of torch-light illumined the darkness around while a band of forty-men advanced two abreast from the opposite extremity of the grove. "These," said Ned in a low tone, "are our helpmates." A smile of anticipated Triumph lighted up Arthurs features as he threw a hasty but penetrating glance over his proposed coadjutors in this desperate undertaking. They formed indeed as wild a group a[s] could be found in the most savage recesses of the Alps or Appenines. Tall & strongly-built with brawny shoulders & sinewy limbs, each might have passed for a model of Hercules or Miletus.[21] Their dress was uniform Doublets & breeches of undressed skin with laced buskins of the same & high sugar-loaf hats[22] from under the broad brims of which dark dishevelled elf-locks straggeled over their bronzed & weather-beaten visages. Their arms were pistols, long-fowling peices, bludgeons & knives of a peculiar form.

When they had reached the place were Arthur stood they made a simultaneous halt & grounded their arms. He returned this civility by a bow & immediately addressed them as follows: "My lads, I feel a just pride in the circumstance of being appointed the captain of so noble a company. fear not that we shall suceed, our arms are stroung & our cause is right, while our antagonist being laden with the burden of treachery & cruelty cannot give full play to those means of defence which he possesses. my directions concerning your conduct shall be summed up in a few words. Be valiant, prudent & secret, & in order to ensure your observance of the latter injunction I require you all to swear by the life of our ancient Patriarch that you will never under any circumstances reveal either the chief or subordinate actors in this night's business. Do you accept the oath?" The answer to this query was a deep & low but energetic & general exclaimation of "We do." "I am satisfied," said Arthur springing to the head of his men. "Now let us depart for time is precious." As he spoke these words The bells of Verdopolis were heard faintly telling the hour of midnight.

They continued their course along the rivers banks shaded from view by the thick foliage which environed them on either side. A dull hollow sound now became audible swelling & dying at intervals as the wind rose or fell. This increased & became steadier as they advanced. Distant lights were also seen glimmering through the trees. Until at length on emerging from the gloom of dark bough's & pendent branches Lord C[aversham's] great mill burst full on their view. It was an immense structure, 100 feet high & two hundred & fifty long. the starlike lamps spangling its vast front & the thunderous roll & incessant crash of its internal machinery, which caused a perceptible trembling of the adjacent ground, Produced such sensations / in the beholder as Milton's Pandemonium[23] could it be realized might inspire. Arthur's eyes kindled as he beheld the huge & lofty edifice, then turning to Ned Laury who stood beside him he said in an animated whisper, "If I am victorious in this undertaking I will call it my first essay in the art of war but mind what I say Ned, it shall not be my last."

In the most perfect silence and order they stole forward expecting every minute to be challenged by the guards who were or ought to have been continually stationed around the mill. however they reached the principal entrance without interruption: the doors were unlocked, the porter's-box was empty & they proceeded to enter the first appartment where such as were not prisoners usually worked. here all was darkness & desertion. they gazed at each other in silent astonishment. "What can all the folk be about?" said one of the men. His question was presently answered by a chorus of voices chanting the following merry stave:

> Let us drive care away
> And laugh while we may
> And sing though it be in the valley of Death
> And still let us drink

    And from wine never shrink
So long my rare lads as our bodies hold Breath

    I'd far rather die
    In good company
Than live a long life with the solemn and sad
    Then let all the world know
    That from toppin[24] to toe
I'm a good roaring fellow a proper, rare lad

    Shouts of laughter followed the conclusion of this Bacchanalian song. The noise evidently procceded from an adjoining room & Ned L[aury] was now deputed by Arthur to learn the occasion of it. He crept softly to the door & on looking through the key-hole perceived a large party consisting of the Guards, overseers & free-labourers of the mill seated round a table which was well furnished with incitements to mirth in the shape of wine-flasks, foaming tankards of old October bottles of whisky & sundry vessels of eau-de-vie & Jamaica rum. At the head of the table was placed a small insignificant figure of a man whom Ned recognized for Captain Tree[25] & who, as well as the rest of the company, appeared to be in a state of considerable elevation. His little cocked nose was glowing like a ruby of the first water & his bleared eyes glimmering & glittering like two farthing candles as he sat embracing with both arms a portly bottle of Potheen[26] almost as large as himself & every now & then giving utterance to such eldri[t]ch screams of laughter as might have appalled the stoutest heart.

    After making his observations / Ned returned to Arthur and informed him how matters stood, adding that the noodles had just drunk themselves to the proper pitch so that they might now all be butchered without trouble. Arthur heard this somewhat barbarous speech with a frown & turning quickly round he said in a commanding tone, "We are not come here to murder a few paltry defenceless underlings but to rescue the oppressed & to wreak vengeance on the head of a treacherous tyrant. I therefore forbid you by virtue of the temporary allegiance you owe me to hurt one hair of those hireling dogs in the next room. You shall merely bind them hand & foot, carry them to the opposite bank of the river, set the prisoners free, fire the mill & then return quietly to your own homes." The men heard these orders with surprise & some little discontent, but they dared not act in opposition to their young leader's express commands. they therefore prepared to carry them into immediate effect.

    thirty of their number headed by Arthur in person proceeded to the banqueting-room, while the remaining ten under Ned Laury's command went towards those upper appartments were the roll & rattle of machinery proclaimed the prescence of the miserable captives whose unceasining labour was ever prolonged "from morn, till dewy eve; from eve, till morn."[27] The convival party were just at the noon of mirth & uproarious fun, shouts of laughter burst from them incessant[l]y. Wine & jokes were going freely round when the folding-doors flew open & our party of armed incendiaries rushed in with a ferocious yell. At this sight of terror some of the boon-companions were instantaneously sobered, but far the greater part had dived much too deeply into their cups to be at all affected by the bodily intrusion of any beings whose substance was as solid & tangible as their own. Accordingly, a general seizure was quickly made. they were bound in couples & conveyed almost unresistingly over the river. it was afterwards discovered however that one of their number, viz C[aptain] Tree, had contrived to make his escape during the confusion. a general search was commenced but it proved unsucessful. the small viper had wriggled out through an unperceived cranny & was no where to be found.

In the midst of these transactions the loud thunder above was suddenly hushed at once & a shrill exhulting cry of joy bursting over-head echoed through the lofty & innumerable appartments of the mill. the heavy tread of many feet was heard descending the principal staircase & Ned Laury now appeared supporting his aged father & followed by upwards of a thousand liberated prisoners. They rushed forward shouting, screaming, & dancing with delight at finding themselves once more free. One of them, whose appearance bespoke him an Englishman, Exclaimed, "where is my deliverer, my saviour? tell me that I may embrace his knees & offer him my life & wealth." "There," said Ned pointing to Arthur. This was a signal for the whole body to spring towards him. his slight frame trembled in the powerful embrace of many a strong sinewy form that for years had been cooped in this massive dungeon for no other crime than that of having in some trifling point opposed a tyrants will or interfered with his pleasures. At length Arthur succeeded in / calming their tumultuous expressions of gratitude. he then enjoined them all to fly instantly from the scene of their sufferings while the cloud of night should yet shield them with its friendly obscurity. Their newly-regained & as yet unenjoyed liberty (except in anticipation) was much too precious to be lightly thrown away & in a few minutes the mill was completely deserted by its former involuntary occupants.

Only the last scene yet remained to be acted. Arthur now commanded his men to light up the piles of greasy waste which lay on the floor around them & this order being obeyed he led them out of the devoted edifice & taking up his station on an adjoining eminence awaited the result. In less than a quater of an hour wreaths of Dun smoke mingled with darting tongues of fire were seen issuing from some of the lower windows. a dull roaring noise was also heard, and after the laspse of another fifteen minutes, the wished for conflagration broke forth at once in a column of clear, red flame which rose suddenly with a rushing sound into the air. It seemed as if this terribly splendid spectacle had been a previously concerted signal for departure. Arthur turned to his band &, after thanking them for the efficient manner in which they had seconded his orders & reminding them of the solemn oath they had taken he bade them all farewell.

A gentle wind was begining to sigh along the river as he re-entered the grove which overhung its waters. the cold clear light of dawn beamed on the eastern skirts of a perfectly cloudless sky. birds were commencing their early morning homage in the dewy-branches above his head & far from the south-west the sea & city sent on the breeze their first matin murmurs. Arthurs mind was not in unison with the fresh awakening loveliness of nature. His eye received the reflection of her rising beauties & his ear heared the soft sweetness of her whispered voice without conveying their impression to his heart. That was too wholly occupied with the delight of gratified vengeance to harbour for an instant any inferior pleasure. A smile curled his beautiful vermillion lips as he thought of Lord C[aversham]'s frantic but useless rage when he should learn the fate of that proud structure whence a full half of his annual revenue was derived & be informed that all the pining captives over whose prolonged torments he had so often gloated were released from his iron grasp & free to breathe the unfettered air of heaven. "Yes," he exclaimed aloud as he followed this train of musing, "Thunderbolt's funeral pile will light the sky for many a long day. I [?swore] mentally that he should be revenged & he has been." "And so shall my lord Caversham," said a shrill voice close beside, & ere he could turn to glance at the speaker the report of a pistol followed and he fell senseless to the earth with an ounce of cold lead in his body. /

CHAPTE.R THE. V.

I must now take an almost Shakesperian licence[28] & represent Arthur to my reader at the distance of nearly two thousand miles from the grove were we left him for dead at the conclusion of the last chapter. Behold him then, lying on a straw pallet under a low-roofed peasant's cabin. the comfortable but limited appartment is as clean & neat as the most scrupulously tidy housewife could desire. A little dresser garnished with polished pewter dishes & well scoured wooden platters occupies one end; at the other a clear bright fire of wood is burning on the clean-swept hearth. A few chairs & three-legged stools are placed at regular distances down the sides & in the midst stands a round deal table covered with a snow-white cloth & ew-platters[29] which seem waiting for the contents of that ample pot now pabbling & hotching[30] on the hearth. Arthurs countenance is almost as pallid as if Death's finger had dried the fresh springs of life in his veins. No transient hue of the rose crosses his white cheek or his still whiter forehead, but A faint crimson still dyes his lips & tells that life has not yet abandoned her citedal. The once transcendent brilliancy of his large dark eyes has faded quite away & given place to the faint languishing lustre of sickness. they are fixed with an expression of touching sadness towards the open door. I hope my reader will deign to glance in the same direction for there a glorious prospect awaits him.

The cabin is situated at the head of a wild glen which is hollowed in the soundless heart of many mountains. on every side they rise clad in the black array of pine-forests like mourning giants. their feet, covered with dark ridgy groves, slope far downward till they almost meet in the centre of the glen. peeping above the gorges which separate their proud summits are dimly seen more distant & loftier hills, some looking darkly & sternly through the thin blue veil of intermediate air, others sparkling in the white robes of snow with which a thousand winters have clothed their hoary forms. Westward the earth-waves roll in long, low billows, glowing gem-like under the glorious light of a fast declining sun which bathes the ocidental air in a sea of celestial radiance. Issuing from this far off & favoured region comes a merry mountain stream, like a messenger of life from heaven, dispensing melody & health through the glen as it glides or dances rapidly along. No tree waves over its brink, except here & there a solitary piine, isolated from the main forest—heath flowers alone & the moss, which covers some huge fragment of grey granite that has rolled down centuries ago from the rocky fells on every side, drink nourishment from its scattered spray. Nothing but the murmurs of this wild rivulet interrupts the solemn silence which pervades earth & sky. An indescribable feeling of mountain calm dwells at this moment on all above, below & around.

But Arthur is not the only inhabitant of this hill-girt cottage: another form sits at the foot of his low bed-stead. it is that / of a young peasant girl apparently about fifteen or sixteen years of age. She is lovely & smiling as a rural Hebë.[31] Her dark shining hair falls in natural curls over a countenance whose rich bloom proclaims health & free communion with the air and light of heaven. large & intensely black eyes impart all the charms of expression to her small but sweetly moulded features, while her dress of dark grey stuff, relieved by a necklace & bracelets of Indian beads, gives an air of mingled modesty & simplicity to the whole contour of her graceful form. This maiden is the daughter & this hut the habitation of Ned Laury. He had heard the report of the pistol from a distance &, apprehensive that some harm might happen to Arthur, had immediately followed in the direction of the sound. On arriving at the grove he beheld the object of his solicitude weltering in a pool of blood. Life to all appearance was totally extinct but in a short time signs of returning animation became visible. Not daring to convey Arthur back to Waterloo Palace in this almost hopeless condition, Ned secreted him for a week in the pot-house before spoken of which formed his lodgings while in Verdopolis, for be it remembered he was not a permanent resident there. At the end of that time as it was become unsafe to remain any longer in the city (the pursuit of the police being now extremely hot after those who were suspected of having originated the late terrible conflagration) He judged it prudent to depart immediately for his distant & retired home, conveying my brother by his own consent with him. But before taking this necessary step Ned had found out after a diligent investigation the person who had attempted Arthur's life. this was no other than Captain Tree, who my readers will recolect had managed to escape on the night of the fire. Shortly after this discovery Captain Tree disappeared & his remains were at length found, gashed with many frightful wounds, by some workmen while they were engaged in cleaning an old drain. At the end of a month

Arthur reached the termination of his long tedious journey. He was now completely exhausted with pain & fatigue. His wounds which had begun to knit were all opened afresh & for three weeks he lay on the straw pallet of the cabin raving in delirious agony. but his fine vigorous constitu[tion] aided by the unremitting & tender care of young Mina Laury triumphed over all; the fever of torment at last subsided & though weak as a newborn infant he began slowly to recover. At this crisis of affairs I presented him to my reader at the opening of the present chapter.

It was as I have said evening. Ned had gone out to hunt early in the afternoon & Mina was left alone with her patient. she was quite unacquainted with his rank & knew him only as a sick & helpless stranger, but his uncommon beauty which still shone pre-eminent in spite of pain & illness, & the superiority of his manner & the gentle tones of his voice when he addressed her, awakened in Mina's heart feelings of wonder & delight. She considered it an honour to be allowed to yield him all the little attentions in her power And thought herself amply rewarded, for the many nights of sleepless watching & days of mournful anxiety she had passed on his / account, by the first ray of returning reason which illumined his dark lustrous eyes.

On this evening they had both remained in profound silence for upwards of an hour, Arthur intently gazing at the setting sun & Mina busily employed with her needle. Just as the golden rim of Appollo's chariot vanished from sight Arthur exclaimed, "Now the sun has disappeared & I shall claim your promise of a song." "I will grant it this minute," replied she raising her head, "If you will lie still & not keep turning round so." "Well my little physician your directions shall be observed, now begin. I am sure you will sing sweetly from the formation of you[r] mouth." Mina smiled and blushed at this delicate compliment & then after informing him that the title of the song was "the fallen soldier's hymn", She sang the following Stanzas in a voice the exquistie melody of whose tones struck the ear the more forcibly from its being wholly destitute of the affectation of art.

> Almighty hush the dying cries
>   That sound so sadly in mine ear
>   The sobs, the groans, the soul-breathed sighs
>   And wipe away the burning tear
>   That now wets many a gallant cheek
>   While pain wrings forth, the wild death-shriek
>   From brave hearts steeled to fear

> Voice of the solemn trumpet sound
> Rend your dark mist-veil from the sky
> Peirce through the war-shouts bursting round
> And swell again triumphantly
> For I would leave this mangl'ed clay
> And pass to regions far-away
>   'Mid lanes of victory
>
> List to that sweet, heart-stirring strain
> That clear, but martial harmony
> It peals above the battle plain
> Like music o'er a stormy sea
> Soothes the wild waves of fear to rest
> And wakes in ev'ry fainting breast
>   A sudden energy
>
> All the dark pageantry of war
> Is fading swiftly from my sight
> The clash of arms sound faint and far
> Death's wing's spread o'er me blackest night
> Yet still that music floats around
> And mingles with its harp-like sound
>   A more than trumpet night /
>
> A flood of light bursts from the skies
> While higher swells that symphony
> I see the Isles of Paradise
> Rise beauteous from a golden sea
> And now I feel the fragrant breeze
> Borne from sweet Eden's bowers & trees
>   Which bloom eternally
>
> Bretheren in arms a long farewell
> To other brighter scenes I go
> Where joys unmixed & endless dwell
> And where undying waters flow
> There I shall bathe in seas of life
> Unharmed by war unvexed by strife
>   Far from this world of woe

As the last note dyed sweetly but mournfully away, Arthur exclaimed with evident astonishment, "Where could you—possibly have heard the words of that song Mina?" "Why," said she, "In a deep & wide valley about ten miles from this & beyond the nearest of those western mountains there is a very splendid palace, the residence of a certain beautiful & great lady. Whenever my father goes on his long journies she sends for me to her house & I live there as a servant till he returns. Once when I was there I happened to be dusting one of the rooms & found this song written on a piece of paper lying under a cabinet. I liked it so much that after once or twice reading over it fastened on my memory & though it is two or three years since I can still remember it word for word." "You are a very clever little girl," replied Arthur smiling, "but what is the name of this great lady?" Just as Mina was about to reply they were both startled by a sudden, sharp, quick growl & at the same instant an immense tigress sprang in through the open door-way. she lighted on Arthurs bed. he made a feeble effort to rise but sank back again from sheer weakness, saying in a faint tone, "Fly Mina save yourself." And now according to all human calculation his days on earth were numbered & Death which had hovered over him so long was about finally to secure his prey. But Mina, roused by the tremendous danger of one whose life was dearer to her than she herself till that moment knew, animated with a courage & prescence of mind alike unusual to her age or sex, seized a large knife which lay on the table & springing forward buried it in the monster's side to the very hilt. Happily she had struck a vital part. the tigress imediately rolled on to the floor wrestled awhile convulsively with death & then lay motionless & rigid. When Mina had a little recovered from her terror she advanced to the bed-side. Arthur held out his hand to her as she approached & taking hers said with energy, "Noble / girl, you have now twice saved my life. your heroic conduct shall be rewarded. you will not find me ungrateful." When they had leisure to reflect, they could not help wondering at the ease with which the ferocious animal had been over-come but on examination it was discovered that she had previously received four or five wounds in various parts of her body.

Steps were now heard rapidly approaching the door & Ned Laury entered with a countenance of horror, crying out, "Were are ye. are ye both devoured, Arthur, Mina, is any life still left in your bodies? if there is, speak." "We are perfectly safe father," answered Mina pointing to the dead tigress. It was some time before Ned's overflowing joy would allow him to speak rationally, but at last he told them that he had roused the beast from her den among the mountains & had been hunting her ever since the morning; that she had several times stood at bay & had as often turned tail again at the discharge of a musket; that a[t] length bothe he & his companions had despaired of setting her for that day & were preparing to relinquish the chase when she suddenly turned & fled in the direction of his cottage. my reader is already made acquainted with the catastrophe which followed this manoeuvre.

A party of about twenty hunters now arrived. they were men who like Ned resided in those retired glens which lay embosomed among the vast &, except by them, untrodden solitudes of the hills, & whose precarious subsistence principally depended on their skill as marksmen, their fleetness of foot & capability of enduring fatigue. Ned invited them to take shelter under his roof for the night. this offer they gladly accepted & a fire being lighted in an adjoining out-house thither they all adjourned. Mina provided them a plentiful & savoury supper from the contents of the pot before mentioned, & Ned produced from a secret recess several choice flasks of mountain-dew.[32]

Mina, having thus supplied the wants of her fathers guests & completed the arrangement of household affairs for the night, retired to her little chamber & soon lost in oblivious sleep all remembrance of the external world. Arthur, thus left alone, watched for sometime the flickering embers now dying on the hearth & the still moonlight stealing through his window. Voices of rude revelry were heard without at intervals vexing the nights dull ear, sometimes with peals of laughter & sometimes with snatches of wild drinking songs. as the wind rose or fell they sounded now close at hand & then borne far-away to almost inaudible distance. Thus he lay for hours revolving in his mind many & perplexing subjects of thought till, wearied out by a train of musing which failed to conduct him to any satisfactory termination, he at last began to feel the hand of Somnus weighing down his eyelids, & resigning himself to the influence of that drowsy power he soon travelled many leagues into the land of Nod. strange to say his dreams that night were filled with images of pretty peasant girls. /

CHAP. THE VI

In a few weeks Arthur, by dint of good nursing & clear air, entirely recovered from the effects of his wounds. He now daily accompanied Ned Laury on his hunting expeditions & thus attained that unerring skill as a marksman & chasseur for which he is so eminently distinguished. The free atmostphere he breathed & the constant exercise he took nerved his limbs & more fully developed his finely proportioned form. Indeed, I think that had it not been for this sojourn among the mountains, he would never have reached that lofty heroic stature & free, bold, chivalric bearing which he now possesses. his features also assumed a richer & sunnier tone of colouring in exchange for the delicate transparent complexion which had before given him a very effiminate appearance. At this period too the fountain of song, whence such mighty streams have since flowed, arose in his heart: the inspiring grandeur of those mountain prospects among which he dwelt waked it & the shadow of their sad though sublime desolation threw over it that dark solemn cloud & roused that mournful voice which is heard & seen in all his strains.

But my reader will perhaps inquire what detained him in a country so distant from all his connections. I will answer briefly & satisfactorily: it was "Love." Yes the proud, Aristocratic, high-minded, refined, elegant Marquis of Douro had actually fallen in love with a poor low-born Peasant's Daughter! & his affection was not unanswered. Mina indeed could not be said so much to love as to worship him. he appeared to her in the light of a superior being, as an angel, an archangel, & a species of awe filled her mind whenever she looked at him.

Such was the state of affairs when Arthur & Ned L[aury] one sultry afternoon were sitting down to rest themselves in a lone hollow among the hills after the successful pursuit of an Indian Antelope.[33] Arthur had long been watching for a favourable moment to ask Ned's consent to an immediate union with his daughter & he now determined that the present opportunity should not be lost. accordingly he began by demanding if Ned did not think that he was now fully competent to gain his living by hunting. The answer was a prompt affirmative. "Well then," continued he, "I am determined to give up my friends, my rank, my title, my wealth & all my prospects in life & dwell for ever in this wild region on condition that you will reward me with your daughter Mina's hand." Honest Ned, who till this instant had not entertained the fragment of an idea concerning Arthur's indiscreet partiality, could not contain his astonishment at a proposal so unexpected. he sat staring for ten minutes as if his eyes would have started from their sockets, muttering all the while, "the lad's gone clean mad; mad as a march hare, mad as a wounded lion." At length as if suddenly recollecting himself he said in an altered tone, "Why Arthur, you've so ta'en me by surprise that I can't give you just a right sort of an answer today. you must wait till to-morrow morning & then I shall have considered the matter better." And with this reply my brother was obliged to be satisfied.

Next morning Ned did not appear at breakfast & Arthur on inquiry found that he had departed at sunrise for the great Palace behind the hill & would not return till noon. / He passed the morning in a state of feverish expectation trying to while away the hours by wandering about the glen. At length perceiving by his curtailed shadow that noon was near he began slowly to retrace his steps. On approaching the hut he was surprised to hear voices in earnest conversation. As he advanced nearer these words, spoken half playfully half seriously in a deep mellow voice whose tones were perfectly familiar to him, were distinctly audible: "So you are the little gipsy who has stolen my son's heart & made him play the truant for so long a time. Ah, I see it will be a difficult task to divide you, but something must be done. this childish affair shall go on no longer."

Arthur sprang forward & in another second stood in my father's presence. after the first warm embrace, prompted by filial & parental love, few words passed on either side. Arthur's were those of strong wild supplication, my father's those of storm & brief command. at length as Ned L[aury], who had returned & was standing near, an u[n]moved spectator, approached to separate his weeping daughter from Arthur, he [Arthur] drew a loaded pistol from his belt & swore that he would blow out the first man's brains who should lay a finger on her. Mina now swooned & fell senseless at his feet. My father looked at his refractory son with an eye which spoke more of sorrow than of anger & calmly advancing he wrested the pistol from his hand, fired it into the air & flung it away. then seizing him strongly in his arms he conveyed him to the carriage which had been brought round to the hut-door, placed him unresistingly within & entering after him ordered the coachman to drive off. After a rapid drive of little more than an hour's duration the carriage stopped at the gate of a splendid mansion.

Arthur had been living all this time unknown to himself in my father's dominions, less than ten miles from his person, for this was one of his country palaces & the same Mina had mentioned as the residence of a certain Great lady who was no other than my mother.[34] here she had found the song which had so much astonished Arthur, for he recognized in it a peice of his own composition. Ned Laury had winked a[t] Arthur's continued abscence from home & neglected to lodge any information against him because he thought it was a fine thing for a young nobleman to breathe a little mountain air & learn the business of a man, i.e. hunting & shooting, without being bothered by books & droning tutors; but when he heard Arthur's proposal of marriage with his daughter he, nobly unmindful of his own interest, determined imediately to inform my father. for this purpose he had left the cottage early in the morning. the result of his communication I have already related & now I have only to say how the lovers bore their final separation.

Arthur for a long time continued to gloom & lower, & fret & pine away, till he became mere skin and bone. But time the great Physician did not vainly apply his balsam to his broken & bleeding heart, and an angel completed the cure. this was—but "Oh no we never mention her." Suffice it to say that the bright & beautiful creature on whose brow my brother has lately placed his coronet[35] quite effaced / the remembrance of Simple Mina Laury. that wild little daisy could not stand before a flower so fair, so elegant & so highly cultured; & accordingly it quickly shrunk into the obscurity of its own green leaves. With Mina the case was rather different. the light of her eyes seemed taken away when Arthur left her. all her stock of warm affections wa[s] centered in him & their sudden separation was a blow not to be lightly got over. for weeks & months she drooped & withered, & poor Ned daily expected to see the cloud of death darken his dwelling. but happily my dear mother became acquainted with the whole affair. she instantly sent for Mina to the Palace. Here, under the influence of gentle attention & sympathetic kindness, she slowly recovered & is at this moment as pretty & blooming, though not quite as merry, as ever.

May 1st   Charlotte Brontë
   1833

EXPLANATORY NOTES

1. *Bud*: Captain John Bud, "the greatest prose writer" among the Young Men of the early Glass Town. Charlotte first describes him in "Characters of the Celebrated Men of the Present Time," 17 December 1829, although he appears earlier in "Blackwoods Young Mens Magazine," December (second issue) 1829. Branwell assumes the name of Captain John Bud for the authorship of "The History of the Young Men," 15 December 1830—7 May 1831.

2. *flashmen*: "A bully to a bawdy house. A whore's bully." *The 1811 Dictionary of the Vulgar Tongue*, reprinted with a foreword by Robert Cromie (Chicago, 1971).

3. *Repentant Prodigal*: Luke 11:11–32

4. *Waterloo-Palace*: The Verdopolitan residence of the Duke of Wellington.

5. *Mr Rundell*: Lord Charles Wellesley's "worthy, learned, ever-to-be-respected and never-to-be-forgotten tutor" (see "Visits in Verreopolis," vol. 1).

6. *Caversham*: Colonel George Frederick, Baron of Caversham. This is Caversham's first appearance in the juvenilia and we learn in "A Day Abroad," written the following year, that he is a villainous associate of Alexander Percy, who murdered Caversham's father in a duel at Percy Hall.

7. *Thunderbolt*: cf. Charlotte's description of the horse, and its name, with Job 39:19–20.

8. *unextinguishable laughter*: A characteristic Homeric phrase; used also in "Noctes Ambrosianae," *Blackwood's Edinburgh Magazine*, 1822–1835.

9. *rare lad*: A term of approbation used loosely by the Glass Town "heavies" to refer both to themselves and to others, usually those destined to be the victims of their midnight body-snatching raids; see Charlotte's "An Interesting Passage in the Lives of Some eminent men of the Present time," and Branwell's "Letters from an Englishman," vol. 1.

10. *"vexed the dull ear of night"*: cf. *King John*, act 3, sc. 4, line 109; and *Henry V*, act 4, prologue, line 11.

11. *rare apes*: "rare lads."

12. *the stumpy, the blunt*: Slang words for money. They occur together in *Lights and Shades of English Life: From the New Monthly Magazine* (Philadelphia: Carey, Lea & Carey, 1828), 2:7. "He inquired whether I had any other dibbs, any more blunt or stumpy, any more money."

13. *Sir John Barleycorn*: A personification of malt-liquor, popularized by Robert Burns in "Tam o' Shanter."

14. *Somnus*: The Roman god of sleep.

15. *dishing some flat*: Slang for cheating or baffling a gull or silly fellow.

16. [*?s.o.t.*]: Although the letters in the manuscript appear to be "s.o.t.," Charlotte may have meant to write "£. s. d."

17. *Lady Dunsandle*: A minor member of Verdopolitan society. Her husband, Lord Dunsandle, appears in an earlier manuscript at a gathering in Bravey's Hotel, the Verdopolitan Gentlemen's Club (see "Visits in Verreopolis," vol. 1).

18. *Lieutenant Tree*: Probably Sergeant Tree, chief bookseller and publisher for Verdopolis.

19. *snob*: "A person belonging to the ordinary or lower classes of society; one having no pretensions to rank or gentility" (*OED*).

20. *spanging*: Springing, leaping, bounding; moving rapidly (*OED*). Scots and Northern dialect, often used by Scott.

21. *Miletus*: A son of Apollo who, after trying to dethrone Minos, founded a city named for himself. Ovid mentions Miletus's pride in his own youthful strength (*Metamorphoses*, Book IX).

22. *sugar-loaf hat*: "A conical hat, pointed, rounded or flat at the top, worn during the Tudor and Stuart periods and after the French Revolution" (*OED*). Here Charlotte is possibly associating it with revolutionaries.

23. *Milton's Pandemonium*: *Paradise Lost*, 1:756; 10:424. The word "Pandemonium" was first used by Milton as the name of the principal city in Hell.

24. *toppin*: Head (dialectical).

25. *Captain Tree*: One of Verdopolis's chief authors and a contributor to the "Young Mens Magazine." Charlotte's next manuscript, "The Green Dwarf," traces the origins of Captain Tree.

26. *Potheen*: "Whiskey distilled in Ireland in small quantities, privately, i.e. the produce of an illicit still" (*OED*).

27. "*from morn, till dewy eve; from eve, till morn*": cf. *Paradise Lost*, 1:742–3.

28. *Shakesperian licence*: Shakespeare's disregard for the unity of place.

29. *ew-platters*: Plates made of yew wood.

30. *pabbling & hotching*: Bubbling and heaving (Scots and Northern dialect).

31. *Hebë*: Greek goddess of youth and cup-bearer to the gods, she had the power of restoring youth and vigor to gods and men.

32. *mountain-dew*: Scotch whiskey; formerly that from illicit stills hidden away in the mountains. The Scottish equivalent of Potheen.

33. *Indian Antelope*: "Indian" used to mean "exotic"; frequently used to describe the African scene, e.g. "I dwelt mid Indian bowers" (see "A Fragment," 11 July 1831).

34. *my mother*: Lady Catherine Wellington, closely modeled on the real Duke of Wellington's wife, Kitty Pakenham.

35. *bright and beautiful creature on whose brow my brother has lately placed his coronet*: Marian Hume, daughter of Sir Alexander Hume Badey; modeled on Elizabeth Hume, eldest daughter of Dr. John Robert Hume, surgeon to the real Duke of Wellington. In the juvenilia, Marian is always presented as "an angel" and ideal heroine: hence, Lord Charles's half-mocking attitude toward her "preciousness" here.

DELETIONS AND CORRECTIONS IN THE MANUSCRIPT

The following deletions and corrections made by Charlotte Brontë in the MS of *Something about Arthur* are keyed to the page and line in which they occur in this edition. The deletions and corrections include all substantive variants. Thirty-five minor changes in spelling made by Charlotte in the course of the writing are not included, since these involve merely the substitution of one letter for another. For example, on page 43, line 11, the second *c* of *accused* is written over a *u*.

The following symbols are employed:

⟨ ⟩ Deleted in MS
[ ] Added in MS
⟨[ ]⟩ An addition subsequently deleted
[⟨ ⟩] A deletion made within an addition

All conjectural readings are indicated by a question-mark within the brackets. Where Charlotte's addition is written on top of the preceding deletion, this is indicated by having the [ ] printed directly against the ⟨ ⟩; where the addition is written above the deletion in the MS, the [ ] is separated from the ⟨ ⟩.

p. 31, l. 14: another, ⟨I⟩ my precarious
p. 31, l. 16: merry tales as my ⟨humerous⟩ [tragic & comic] powers
p. 31, l. 24: Vice furnishe⟨d⟩[s]
p. 32, l. 2: verses My ⟨comp⟩ [shape] still
p. 32, l. 5: fair. ⟨And⟩ Nature
p. 32, l. 10: observation. ⟨a⟩ circumstances
p. 32, l. 15: education the ⟨comforts.⟩ pleasures
p. 32, l. 17: Truth must be ⟨sp⟩ spoken
p. 32, l. 18: confession) ⟨Some⟩ [two] of the
p. 32, l. 23: In my mind ⟨lik⟩ as
p. 32, l. 29: but the ⟨strong⟩ [keen] cravings
p. 32, l. 34: I set off ⟨in the⟩ strengthened
p. 33, l. 3: After ⟨h⟩[r]eceiving
p. 33, l. 5: demands of ⟨Nature⟩ of ⟨my⟩ [a perfectly] ravenous
p. 33, l. 9: previous hardships ⟨alone⟩

p. 33, l. 25: But ⟨capr⟩ Charles
p. 33, l. 27: I expect you to ⟨retu⟩ fall
p. 33, l. 31: seated at ⟨the⟩ his desk
p. 33, l. 32: as ⟨f⟩ he testified
p. 34, l. 1: said I with ⟨my⟩ [a] low⟨est⟩ bow
p. 34, l. 12: forgotten ⟨it⟩ Arthurs
p. 34, l. 17: motto was ⟨now⟩ [for the present]
p. 34, l. 19: I am not ⟨res⟩ under
p. 34, l. 22: at th⟨at⟩[is] age
p. 34, l. 24: brown curling ⟨curling⟩ hair
p. 34, l. 28: living ⟨person⟩ ⟨[man]⟩ thing besides
p. 34, l. 29: How often ⟨have I feared &⟩ [when thwarted &] provoked
p. 34, l. 34: self-controul ⟨how long will⟩ I'll allow you
p. 35, l. 1: title of ⟨Viscount⟩ Colonel
p. 35, l. 2: who could carry ⟨his⟩ an overdose
p. 35, l. 6: almost as ⟨strong⟩ [ardent] as it ⟨a⟩[i]s now
p. 35, l. 8: Universe & ⟨loved⟩ [regarded] it with
p. 35, l. 9: proportioned to his ⟨high⟩ [lofty] estimate
p. 35, l. 9: He ⟨often⟩ used to
p. 35, l. 14: as an arow while ⟨his charger⟩ [Thunderbolt, (his charger's name)] reared
p. 35, l. 15: performed the demi-volte⟨d⟩
p. 35, l. 18: happened that ⟨there was to be⟩ a grand
p. 35, l. 22: Thunderbolt should ⟨th⟩ not have
p. 35, l. 24: accrue to the ⟨winning horse⟩ conqueror
p. 35, l. 27: he had just ⟨received⟩ [obtained]
p. 35, l. 28: he received a ⟨prompt⟩ [cheerful] and
p. 35, l. 32: himself ⟨alone on some⟩ at a distance
p. 35, l. 33: a look at the ⟨vast⟩ huge
p. 35, l. 37: sitting alone ⟨on t the⟩ [at the bottom of the] vast
p. 35, l. 39: After ⟨an⟩ [a short but] anxious
p. 36, l. 2: trumpets & a ⟨lo⟩ sky-rending
p. 36, l. 6: half the ⟨course⟩ [race] was run
p. 36, l. 10: mingled with ⟨loud⟩ exclamations
p. 36, l. 11: My father who was ⟨among the spectators⟩ [seated with the other] Sovereigns
p. 36, l. 12: anxiously ⟨down⟩ [down]
p. 36, l. 14: meantime the ⟨race⟩ victory
p. 36, l. 17: the foot of the ⟨S⟩ throne

p. 36, l. 19: round ⟨his⟩ its neck
p. 36, l. 20: assembly. ⟨The⟩ In a few hours
p. 36, l. 26: on the moon ⟨which⟩ now beginning
p. 36, l. 32: to turn ⟨tai⟩ [his back] in so ⟨ludicrous⟩ [contemp⟨t⟩uous]
p. 36, l. 36: moonlight and ⟨regerading⟩ ⟨regarding him⟩ as he leant
p. 36, l. 37: well-polished fowling peice ⟨with a pai⟩ regarding him
p. 36, l. 37: dark eyes ⟨that not a little⟩ [whose expression] of earnest curiosity ⟨that⟩ not
p. 37, l. 3: induces you to ⟨make me the⟩ [offer me] your assistance
p. 37, l. 6: concerned ⟨at⟩ [on account] as I suppose
p. 37, l. 10: been ⟨dreadf⟩ wickedly
p. 37, l. 11: tha⟨he⟩[t] no horse
p. 37, l. 14: if you can⟨?do so⟩ [show] me
p. 37, l. 17: Caversham ⟨is⟩ [has been] the main⟨?spring of that cheatary⟩ [hand in this cheatary]
p. 37, l. 24: pumped by ⟨one who⟩ [a man of] understanding
p. 37, l. 33: murderer⟨s⟩[&]
p. 37, l. 37: I ha⟨d⟩[ve] my reasons
p. 37, l. 39: borne to ⟨have⟩ see⟨n⟩ him ⟨life⟩ [live] disgraced
p. 38, l. 2: but ⟨do⟩ we are going
p. 38, l. 2: dishonoured ⟨my la⟩ have you
p. 38, l. 3: enter into ⟨my⟩ [the] motives
p. 38, l. 5: Well ⟨I am⟩ the horse
p. 38, l. 8: Laury" ⟨Wher⟩ Do you reside
p. 38, l. 10: What ⟨do th⟩ name
p. 38, l. 14: who ⟨could⟩ [can] not write
p. 38, l. 15: white-handed ⟨for on⟩ "Very-well
p. 38, l. 16: what you like." ⟨After⟩ this agreement
p. 38, l. 18: The moon was ⟨shedding a sickly light f⟩ [beaming with sickly lustre] in a sky
p. 38, l. 19: indistinct aspect ⟨which⟩ [that] added
p. 38, l. 23: night and ⟨of rest⟩ [sleep]
p. 38, l. 30: instant ⟨a⟩ [the] red glow of fire-light ⟨sh⟩ ⟨bea⟩ streamed
p. 38, l. 32: sign was a ⟨fair tankard of⟩ [monkey holding] in one hand
p. 39, l. 2: he wishe⟨s⟩[d]
p. 39, l. 11: accordingly ⟨he⟩ lep⟨t⟩[ing] through the ⟨narrow⟩ [small]
p. 39, l. 12: he found himself in ⟨th⟩ a long
p. 39, l. 23: if more is ⟨re⟩ wanted
p. 39, l. 23: Come ⟨that's⟩ [there's] a smart 'un

p. 39, l. 26: admonish⟨ing⟩ [ed] his guest
p. 39, l. 26: the dainties ⟨suspended⟩ so tempttingly
p. 39, l. 29: a ⟨long⟩ [large] low roofed ⟨place⟩ appartment
p. 39, l. 31: wooden benches ⟨seven or⟩ eight men
p. 39, l. 32: ample ⟨portions⟩ [draughts] of the potent
p. 40, l. 20: the laugh now ⟨circul⟩ went
p. 40, l. 23: cousin thus, ⟨at⟩[W]ell Jerry
p. 40, l. 24: I ⟨whi⟩ wish
p. 40, l. 25: I ⟨don⟩ daresay
p. 40, l. 31: enough to do ⟨for⟩ himself
p. 40, l. 36: fine black Ar⟨b⟩ab
p. 41, l. 2: promising method ⟨which would⟩ [of tying ⟨as⟩] as it were
p. 41, l. 6: answered ⟨to⟩ my ⟨satisfaction⟩ highest expectations
p. 41, l. 13: after recommened⟨ed⟩ [ing] his cousin
p. 41, l. 14: attentions ⟨proceede⟩ [hastened] ⟨to claim to the promised recompense⟩ to discover
p. 41, l. 18: took possession of & ⟨d⟩[w]ent away
p. 42, l. 2: given ⟨in hon⟩ [by] Lady Dunsandle ⟨in honnour of⟩ [on the occasion of] the races
p. 42, l. 8: Lord Caversham ⟨was⟩ [was young] and a bachelor
p. 42, l. 10: the excitement⟨s⟩
p. 42, l. 12: Douro. ⟨All⟩ Every
p. 42, l. 15: words. ⟨Mad⟩ "you will
p. 42, l. 26: moment ⟨turning⟩ [assuming] an ashy paleness
p. 42, l. 27: Dog" ⟨exclaimed⟩ [replied] Arthur
p. 42, l. 28: I ⟨give⟩ [blow] you
p. 42, l. 29: retorted ⟨his Lords⟩ [C.]
p. 42, l. 30: thus to me ⟨Awa⟩ [Off] this instant
p. 42, l. 31: confusion ⟨many⟩ ⟨one⟩ ladies
p. 43, l. 6: my brother ⟨revealed to⟩ [set forth his] mean
p. 43, l. 10: fire-arms ⟨or⟩ [as] he in his wisdom
p. 43, l. 12: of ⟨tramping⟩ [tampering] with
p. 43, l. 13: Arthur ⟨wi⟩ smilling disdainfully
p. 43, l. 16: sooner ⟨suff⟩ [burn] my patent
p. 43, l. 17: it would be a ⟨great⟩ [greet] sheeme
p. 43, l. 21: springing ⟨on him⟩ [forward] he ⟨tripped up his h⟩ [dashed him] furiously
p. 43, l. 23: squirting out to ⟨such good⟩ [in a stream] of black blood
p. 44, l. 2: a corpse ⟨his⟩ life

p. 44, l. 6: dread to supernatural ⟨exertions⟩ efforts
p. 44, l. 6: pillar ⟨clung with⟩ clasped
p. 44, l. 8: excited by rage as he ⟨with⟩ [by] dread
p. 44, l. 9: success. ⟨An⟩ Lord
p. 44, l. 13: a livid ⟨hue stained the⟩ [crimson glowed] in their blood ⟨stained⟩ [streaked] visages
p. 45, l. 2: Arthur⟨'s breath was⟩ recovered
p. 45, l. 7: sick-bed now ⟨came upon him⟩ awoke again
p. 45, l. 9: One evening he ⟨had been⟩ [after] sitting
p. 45, l. 10: means of ⟨a⟩[g]ratifying
p. 45, l. 10: revenge ⟨that⟩ which consumed
p. 45, l. 12: walk [⟨ed⟩ out] on the terrace ⟨?to can⟩ [of Waterloo Palace]
p. 45, l. 14: its wispers with ⟨e⟩ the sound
p. 45, l. 16: floated gaily ⟨down.⟩ [on its] heaving bosom
p. 45, l. 17: dim & fading ⟨?perfu⟩ splendor
p. 45, l. 17: still faintly ⟨suff⟩ [illumined] every
p. 45, l. 21: Gruff voice ⟨which⟩ exclaiming
p. 45, l. 26: months since ⟨?3 *words* you did no⟩ [I believe the thing did not] quite answer
p. 45, l. 27: come to ⟨tell you⟩ [say] that there's another
p. 45, l. 31: remember ⟨I t⟩ my reason
p. 46, l. 1: had ⟨done⟩ ⟨inju⟩ done you some injury
p. 46, l. 8: business. ⟨But before⟩ ⟨[we go]⟩ I must premise
p. 46, l. 17: Town. ⟨As⟩ [When] they entered
p. 46, l. 18: the river as it ⟨flowed⟩ stole
p. 46, l. 20: around ⟨as⟩ while
p. 46, l. 26: the most savage ⟨regio⟩ recesses
p. 46, l. 29: skin with ⟨lac⟩ [laced] buskins
p. 46, l. 34: When they ⟨were come near the⟩ [had reached] the place
p. 47, l. 4: ancient Patriarch ⟨that⟩ that you
p. 47, l. 9: "⟨Time is⟩ Now let us
p. 47, l. 17: immense structure ⟨20⟩ 100 feet
p. 47, l. 20: Produced ⟨sen⟩ [such] sensations
p. 47, l. 23: Laury ⟨he⟩[w]ho stood
p. 47, l. 24: If I am ⟨s⟩[v]ictorious
p. 47, l. 28: guards who ⟨are or⟩ were or ought
p. 48, l. 14: incitements to ⟨drinking⟩ [mirth]
p. 48, l. 16: At the head of the table was ⟨seat⟩ placed
p. 48, l. 19: His ⟨sm⟩ little cocked nose

p. 48, l. 22: as large as himself & ⟨often as⟩ every now
p. 48, l. 26: adding that the ⟨b⟩[n]oodles
p. 48, l. 28: trouble ⟨If⟩ Arthur heard
p. 48, l. 29: he said ⟨?We are here to save *1 word* t⟩ in a commanding tone
p. 49, l. 3: the prescence of ⟨those⟩ [the] miserable
p. 49, l. 6: laughter ⟨rose⟩ burst ⟨?th⟩ from
p. 49, l. 8: ferocious yell. At⟨t⟩ this sight
p. 49, l. 10: cups to ⟨be driven⟩ be at all
p. 49, l. 16: search was ⟨immediately⟩ commenced
p. 49, l. 17: to be found. ⟨The⟩ In the midst
p. 49, l. 19: & a ⟨loud⟩ shrill
p. 49, l. 27: This was ⟨the⟩ [a] signal for the whole body to ⟨rush⟩ [spring]
p. 49, l. 29: in the ⟨massive grasp⟩ ⟨[of sinewy &]⟩ [powerful embrace of many a] strong sinewy form
p. 49, l. 30: no other ⟨reason⟩ [crime] than
p. 49, l. 32: calming ⟨this⟩ [their] tumultuous
p. 49, l. 38: involuntary occup⟨at⟩ants
p. 49, l. 39: Arthur ⟨desired⟩ [now] commanded
p. 50, l. 1: his men to ⟨blow⟩ light up
p. 50, l. 3: result. ⟨A⟩[I]n less
p. 50, l. 4: darting ⟨d⟩[t]ongues
p. 50, l. 7: conflagration broke ⟨fo⟩ forth
p. 50, l. 8: rose suddenly ⟨in⟩ with
p. 50, l. 13: begining to sigh ⟨over⟩ along
p. 50, l. 16: far ⟨to⟩ [from] the south-west
p. 50, l. 19: reflection of ⟨y⟩[h]er
p. 50, l. 25: a full half of his ⟨inc⟩ annual revenue
p. 50, l. 27: gloated were ⟨?*3 words*⟩ [released from his iron grasp &] free
p. 51, l. 4: were we left ⟨y⟩ him
p. 51, l. 5. lying ⟨under⟩ [on] a straw ⟨cabin⟩ [pallet] under
p. 51, l. 12: snow-white ⟨table-⟩ cloth & ⟨d⟩[e]w-platters
p. 51, l. 13: of ⟨a⟩[t]hat ample pot
p. 51, l. 16: forehead. but A⟨n⟩ faint crimson
p. 51, l. 18: dark eyes ⟨is⟩ [has] faded
p. 51, l. 20: sadness ⟨in the⟩ towards
p. 51, l. 24: their feet cov⟨r⟩ered
p. 51, l. 25: downward ⟨and⟩ [till they] almost meet
p. 51, l. 30: earth-waves roll ⟨ov⟩ in long low billows glowing ⟨with⟩

p. 52, l. 2: health through⟨t⟩ the glen
p. 52, l. 3: waves ⟨on⟩ [over] its brink
p. 52, l. 6: drink ⟨waters⟩ nourishment
p. 52, l. 8: interrupts ⟨their⟩ [the] solemn
p. 52, l. 9: mountain ⟨stillness⟩ [calm] ⟨?dense⟩ dwells
p. 52, l. 14: smiling as a ⟨heebie⟩ [rural] Hebë
p. 52, l. 15: whose rich ⟨sunny⟩ bloom
p. 52, l. 18: relieved by a ⟨neck⟩ necklace
p. 52, l. 19: simplicity to ⟨her⟩ the whole
p. 52, l. 21: distance & ⟨p⟩[a]pprehensive
p. 52, l. 27: hopeless condition. ⟨He⟩ [Ned] secreted
p. 52, l. 27: for a week⟨s⟩ in the pot-house
p. 52, l. 35: investigation ⟨?his victim⟩ the person
p. 52, l. 37: to escape ⟨de⟩ [on the night of the fire]
p. 53, l. 1: cleaning ⟨out⟩ an old drain
p. 53, l. 4: he lay on ⟨his⟩ the straw
p. 53, l. 9: him to ⟨t⟩[m]y reader
p. 53, l. 10: Ned ⟨L⟩[h]ad
p. 53, l. 17: her power ⟨to bestow⟩ And ⟨considered⟩ [thought] herself
p. 53, l. 17: many ⟨sleep⟩ nights of sleepless
p. 53, l. 19: first ⟨l⟩[r]ay of returning reason ⟨th⟩ which
p. 53, l. 21: they had both ⟨continued in sile⟩ remained
p. 53, l. 22: Arthur intently ⟨wo⟩ gazing
p. 53, l. 37: And ⟨whi⟩ wipe
p. 54, l. 34: There ⟨to⟩ I shall bathe
p. 54, l. 37: last note dye⟨s⟩[d]
p. 55, l. 1: palace the ⟨ho⟩ residence
p. 55, l. 2: my father goes ⟨to⟩ on
p. 55, l. 3: till he returns. On⟨e⟩[ce] ⟨day⟩
p. 55, l. 4: happened to be ⟨do⟩ dusting
p. 55, l. 5: piece of paper ⟨&⟩ lying
p. 55, l. 10: same instant a⟨n⟩ ⟨beautiful⟩ [immense] tigress
p. 55, l. 13: Fly Mina ⟨sa⟩ save
p. 55, l. 17: knew, ⟨scraed⟩ [animated] with
p. 55, l. 18: her age ⟨&⟩ [or] sex
p. 55, l. 20: the tigress ⟨relaxing its grasp⟩ imediately rolled
p. 55, l. 22: recovered from ⟨the⟩ her terror
p. 55, l. 23: said ⟨n⟩[w]ith energy
p. 55, l. 31: entered with a ⟨?1 word⟩ countenance

p. 56, l. 7: skill as mark⟨eress⟩ [smen]
p. 56, l. 9: this offer they ⟨all⟩ [gladly] accepted
p. 56, l. 10: out-house thither⟨er⟩ they all
p. 56, l. 19: his window. ⟨Sounds⟩ [Voices] of ⟨voi⟩ rude
p. 57, l. 4: expeditions & ⟨?soon became⟩ thus attained
p. 57, l. 6: he took nerved ⟨?restored them⟩ his limbs
p. 57, l. 9: never have ⟨recovered⟩ [reached] that
p. 57, l. 11: colouring ⟨than⟩ [in exchange for] the
p. 57, l. 15: the shadow of ⟨that⟩ [their] sad ⟨but⟩ [though] sublime
p. 57, l. 16: solemn cloud & ⟨waked⟩ [roused] that mournful voice
p. 57, l. 21: in love with ⟨N⟩ a poor low-born
p. 57, l. 27: to rest themselves ⟨after t⟩ [in a lone] hollow
p. 58, l. 1: hunting. ⟨Ne⟩) The answer
p. 58, l. 5: till this ⟨moment⟩ [instant] had not
p. 58, l. 7: he ⟨starred⟩ [sat staring] for ten minutes
p. 58, l. 16: behind the hill & ⟨was⟩ [would] not ⟨exp⟩ [return] till noon
p. 58, l. 19: glen ⟨with his gun⟩ At length
p. 58, l. 21: conversation. ⟨On nearer approach he thoug⟩ [As he advanced nearer these] words
p. 58, l. 29: Arthur's were ⟨words⟩ [those] of ⟨the⟩ [strong]
p. 58, l. 34: Mina ⟨s⟩[n]ow swooned
p. 58, l. 37: the air & ⟨thre⟩ [flung] it away
p. 58, l. 39: brought ⟨round⟩ round
p. 59, l. 3: mansion ⟨this was⟩ Arthur
p. 59, l. 5: dominions ⟨so⟩[, l]ess than
p. 59, l. 5: person ⟨t⟩[f]or this
p. 59, l. 6: the same ⟨which⟩ Mina
p. 59, l. 17: related. ⟨Arthur⟩ & now
p. 59, l. 19: continued to ⟨pi⟩ gloom
p. 59, l. 20: Physician ⟨at length he grew wel⟩ [did not vainly apply his balsam to] his broken heart
p. 59, l. 24: coronet ⟨?complet⟩ quite effaced
p. 59, l. 25: could not ⟨?stain⟩ stand before ⟨so fa⟩ a flower so fair so ⟨hi⟩ elegant
p. 59, l. 26: it quickly ⟨?ex⟩ shrunk
p. 59, l. 31: expected to see⟨e⟩ the cloud

ALTERATIONS OF PUNCTUATION

The following is a list of all changes of punctuation. The editor's punctuation comes first, followed by that of the original manuscript.

p. 31, l. 14: another,] another.
p. 31, l. 18: Keepers,] Keepers.
p. 31, l. 18: poachers,] poachers.
p. 31, l. 19: Highwaymen,] Highwaymen.
p. 32, l. 11: men's] men's'
p. 32, l. 14: society,] society.
p. 33, l. 4: Father's] Father's'
p. 33, l. 11: pantaloons,] pantaloons.
p. 33, l. 14: emeralds)] emeralds.
p. 33, l. 29: approvingly] approvingly"
p. 34, l. 11: Indeed] Indeed"
p. 34, l. 32: smile,] smile.
p. 35, l. 1: Caversham,] Caversham.
p. 35, l. 4: jockey,] jockey.
p. 36, l. 7: rivals,] rivals.
p. 36, l. 9: manouvre] manouvre.
p. 36, l. 12: hand,] hand.
p. 36, l. 18: attired,] attired.
p. 36, l. 30: amphitheatre,] amphitheatre.
p. 37, l. 3: assistance?] assistance.
p. 37, l. 7: behaviour."] behaviour".
p. 37, l. 14: How?] How,
p. 37, l. 20: C[aversham],] C.
p. 37, l. 37: say,] say.
p. 38, l. 10: may] "may
p. 38, l. 11: 'Arthur'] "Arthur"
p. 38, l. 19: indistinct] indistinct,
p. 38, l. 22: lanes] lanes.
p. 38, l. 27: chuckle,] chuckle.
p. 38, l. 32: ale,] ale.
p. 38, l. 36: hotel] hotel.

p. 39, l. 1: outhouse, Exclaiming] outhouse. "Exclaiming
p. 39, l. 7: Ned] Ned."
p. 39, l. 8: hesitated,] hesitated.
p. 39, l. 12: him,] him.
p. 39, l. 13: vault,] vault.
p. 39, l. 19: room] room"
p. 40, l. 3: all?] all.
p. 40, l. 17: is] is"
p. 40, l. 30: secret.] secret,
p. 40, l. 38: Aye] Aye"
p. 40, l. 38: sure] sure"
p. 41, l. 9: comunication,] comunication.
p. 42, l. 7: attention,] attention.
p. 42, l. 11: flattery] flattery.
p. 42, l. 15: words,] words.
p. 42, l. 25: C[aversham],] C.
p. 43, l. 5: him,] him.
p. 43, l. 6: room.] room,
p. 43, l. 13: &c. &c.] &c. &c."
p. 44, l. 6: efforts,] efforts.
p. 44, l. 9: C[aversham],] C.
p. 45, l. 11: reflections,] reflections.
p. 45, l. 21: Arthur] Arthur.
p. 45, l. 24: night?] night.
p. 45, l. 32: Thunderbolt?] Thunderbolt.
p. 46, l. 32: were] were,
p. 46, l. 36: follows] follows"
p. 47, l. 16: C[aversham's]] C.
p. 47, l. 18: long.] long,
p. 47, l. 24: whisper,] whisper.
p. 47, l. 32: worked.] worked,
p. 48, l. 26: stood,] stood.
p. 48, l. 28: trouble] trouble"
p. 48, l. 29: tone,] tone.
p. 48, l. 34: river,] river.
p. 49, l. 14: C[aptain]] C.
p. 49, l. 24: One] "One
p. 50, l. 32: ere] 'ere

p. 51, l. 16: forehead,] forehead.
p. 52, l. 27: condition,] condition.
p. 52, l. 32: conflagration)] conflagration,
p. 52, l. 36: life.] life,
p. 53, l. 7: all;] all,
p. 54, l. 37: away,] away.
p. 55, l. 20: part.] part,
p. 55, l. 35: he had] "he had
p. 56, l. 24: thought] thought.
p. 57, l. 19: connections?] connections.
p. 57, l. 26: L[aury]] L.
p. 58, l. 20: steps.] steps,
p. 58, l. 31: L[aury],] L.
p. 59, l. 12: i.e] i.ë
p. 59, l. 17: related] related.

The following emendations have also been made to the manuscript:

p. 31, l. 18: been] beed
p. 33, l. 12: of which] of of which
p. 38, l. 18: in a sky] in a an sky
p. 42, l. 6: flocked round him] flocked round round him
p. 45, l. 9: One evening after] One evening he after
p. 45, l. 23: standing at one] standing at at one
p. 48, l. 34: carry them to] carry them them to
p. 50, l. 13: sigh] sight
p. 51, l. 28: through] throught
p. 57, l. 9: stature & free] stature & & free

LOCATION OF MANUSCRIPTS
by Charlotte and Patrick Branwell Brontë
Referred to in the Introduction and Notes

British Library

Charlotte:

"Blackwoods Young Mens Magazine," December (second issue) 1829; Ashley MS. 157.
"The Foundling. A Tale Of Our Times By Captain Tree," 31 May—27 June 1833; Ashley MS. 159.
"High Life In Verdopolis, or The difficulties of annexing a suitable title to a work practically illustrated in six chapters. By Lord C A F Wellesley," 20 February—20 March 1834; Add. MSS. 34255.
"Speech of His Grace The Duke of Zamorna At the Opening of the First Angrian Parliament," 20 September 1834; Add. MSS. 34255.
"The Spell, An Extravaganza. By Lord Charles Albert Florian Wellesley," 21 June—21 July 1834; Add. MSS. 34255.

Branwell:

"The History of the Young Men," 15 December 1830—7 May 1831; Ashley MS. 187.

Brontë Parsonage Museum

Charlotte:

"Blackwoods Young Mens Magazine," September 1829; S. G. 95.
"A Day at Parry's Palace By Lord Charles Wellesley," 22 August 1830; B85.
"A Fragment," 11 July 1831; B82 and B87.
"The History of the Year," 12 March 1829; B80(11).
"I have now written a great many books," ca. late 1839; B125(1).
"The origin of the O'Deans," 12 March 1829; B80(11).
[Zamorna's Exile, Canto 1] "And when you left me what thoughts had I then," 19 July 1836; B93.

Branwell:

"History of the Rebellion in My Fellows," 1828; No. 112.
"The Monthly Intelligencer," 27 March—25 April 1833; No. 117.

Brotherton Library, Leeds

Branwell:

"Letters from an Englishman," 2 September 1830—2 August 1832.

Ellis Library, University of Missouri—Columbia

Charlotte:

"Lily Hart," 7 November 1833.
"The Secret," ca. 7 November 1833.

Houghton Library, Harvard University

Charlotte:

"The Adventures Of Mon Edouard de Crack   By Lord C Wellesley," 22 February 1830; MS. Lowell 1(3).
"Blackwoods Young Mens Magazine," August 1829; MS. Lowell 1(6).
"An Interesting Passage in the Lives of Some eminent men of the Present time   By Lord Charles Wellesley," 18 June 1830; MS. Lowell 1(1).

Branwell:

"Branwells Blackwoods Magazine," January 1829; MS. Lowell 1(8).

Humanities Research Center, The University of Texas at Austin

Charlotte:

"The Green Dwarf   A Tale Of The Perfect Tense   By Lord Charles Albert Florian Wellesley," 2 September 1833; Stark Collection.
"Something about Arthur   Written by Charles Albert Florian Wellesley," 1 May 1833; Stark Collection.

The Huntington Library

Charlotte:

"A Day Abroad," 15 June 1834; HM. 2577.
"A Peep Into A Picture Book," 30 May 1834; HM. 2577.

New York Public Library

Charlotte:

"The origin of the Islanders," 12 March 1829; Berg Collection.
"Tales of the Islanders By Charlotte Bronte," 12 March—30 July 1830; Berg Collection.

Pierpont Morgan Library

Charlotte:

"The Bridal," 14 July—20 August 1832; Bonnell Collection.
"Last Will And Testament Of Florence Marian Wellesley Marchioness of Douro Duchess Of Zamorna And Princess Of The Blood Of The Twelves," 5 January 1834; Bonnell Collection.
"Passing Events," 21–29 April 1836; MA. 30.
"The Professor," 27 June 1846; MA. 31.

Princeton University Library

Charlotte:

"Emma," 27 November 1853; Taylor Collection.
[Mina Laury] 17 January 1838; Taylor Collection.

Untraceable MSS (Formerly in the Law Collection, Honresfeld, England)

Charlotte:

"Characters of the Celebrated Men of the Present Time. By Captain Tree," 17 December 1829.
"My Angria and the Angrians By Lord Charles Albert Florian Wellesley," 14 October 1834.

"A Romantic Tale By Charlotte Brontë," [15?] April 1829.
"Visits in Verreopolis. By Lord Charles Wellesley. In Two Volumes. Volume First," 7–11 December 1830.

A